WHY LIV?

JON SEBASTIAN SHIFRIN

Contents

Acknowledgements

Why Liv? is inspired by and draws on the work of various political theorists and historians, most notably David Graeber's *Bullshit Jobs: A Theory*, Yuval Noah Harari's *Sapiens: A Brief History of Humankind*, and Richard Rorty's *Achieving Our Country*. Readers keen on a full rendition of these scholars' ideas are encouraged to explore their writing.

Out of the crooked timber of humanity, no straight
thing was ever made.

—Immanuel Kant

PART I

DUSK

CHAPTER 1

MIND OVER MARCY

The Comitans, huddled together like penguins in the Arctic cold, waved posters at passing cars, cheering heartily when one honked in approval. "Guns not Butter," one sign read. Another, "When Liberals Lead, Freedom Bleeds." And, predictably, "I'm John Galt." I nearly ran headlong into them.

Goddammit, I thought. Why now?

The Comitans were a menacing omen. Others existed, of course, like the rain. New York was in the midst of a record, nonstop deluge. Some claimed it was global warming, but most climate models predicted the East Coast would see less rainfall, not more. It had something to do with shifting currents in the Atlantic. Convection, I believe.

Then there was the economic crisis. Nobody could have seen it coming, right? A speculative bubble, evident only after the fact. That's finance. Good years, bad years—the price of prosperity, supposedly. Not really. It was perfectly predictable. The signs were clear.

However, the Comitans were altogether different. After all, you could adjust to the lousy weather, but did it even matter if you went to work? Sunny weather only drove home the cruelty of cubicle captivity. As for the Wall Street-induced economic crisis, sure, it was ruinous, but mostly for those at a comfortable remove. For the wealthy, it was just momentary turbulence in the first-class cabin, a mere hiccup. The rich never paid for their misdeeds; the poor always did, even if blameless.

The Comitans were genuinely frightening and completely impossible to ignore. No sooner had you forgotten about the noisy irritants than a new crop arrived, spewing hate like crazed soccer hooligans and accosting you as you left the grocery store.

At first, I doubted they would ever converge on the city. It was a reasonable expectation given that, initially, they mostly stuck to their southern strongholds, holding rallies in places like Biloxi, Mississippi, and Decatur, Georgia. But then they began to spread, like a toxic contagion.

Although they kept getting closer, it still seemed unlikely they would actually breach the city limits. New York—cosmopolitan, progressive, diverse—personified the evil they detested. Why come at all?

But they did. It was a modern-day sacking of Rome. Thousands converged on Manhattan on chartered buses that discharged them into Midtown, from where they strategically fanned out across the city, heckling and jeering and picking fights like rabid dogs along the way.

I first spotted them in my neighborhood a few weeks ago. After that, my encounters were mostly from a distance, though each time less so. I should have expected the inevitable. After nearly colliding with a dozen or so of the rabble-rousers after turning the corner of Fifty-Second Street, I did what any New Yorker would do when crossing paths with the deranged and possibly dangerous: I stared ahead blankly. Streetwise. That's what Gotham's concrete canyons required.

In my peripheral vision, I caught sight of a seemingly disembodied hand from the huddled mass, finger pointing at me accusingly, and a swarm of sneering faces. Over the music playing on my earbuds, a "fuck you" registered, along with some other choice insults. I did not linger. The rain was getting heavy, and I was late for work.

"Looks like you've seen better days, Liv," Jay said as I staggered into the office, soaked to the bone. On a positive note, I was relieved to have survived my first direct contact with the Comitans unscathed.

"Every day is better than Monday," I sulked.

Jay was the earnest receptionist. Just out of college, he was full of enthusiasm, ambition, and drive. I resisted expressing my cynicism about the corporate grind. Why let on the oasis was a mirage? He would catch on eventually.

"Have a good weekend?" he asked.

"Yeah, you know, the usual." I mimicked injecting myself with a hypodermic needle. Sometimes I couldn't help myself.

I leaned my wet umbrella against the far corner wall of the reception area and walked through two glass doors. Passing a bank of small cubicles, I slowly made my way to my own space situated at the end of the office. After hanging up my wet jacket, I booted my computer. Its groan and flicker immediately began sapping life from me—the price, it seemed, of earning one's keep.

I had just completed culling my in-box and checking the newswire when an automatic reminder popped up on my screen. I'd forgotten about the staff meeting. It normally began at ten but had been pushed up on account of Marcy. My memory lapse was probably my subconscious's doing—I knew what was in store.

I took a deep breath, straightened my tie, and walked to the conference room. My colleagues were already sitting around the rectangular table, requiring me to situate myself in a chair along the far wall. Jay shot me a look of feigned outrage, peering down at his watch. I discreetly gestured another injection.

Mortimer, who headed Marshland Cooper's New York office, kicked off the meeting with a few words of welcome. "You're in for a treat this morning. Without further delay, let me turn this over to Marcy, who has a few announcements about an exciting new initiative. I'm sure that, as ever, her guidance will prove informative. Marcy?"

"Thank you, Morty," Marcy replied with an effortless flip of her hair. "Good morning, everyone. I hope you've had a wonderful weekend. I know I did. I want to talk briefly about what we're calling the Eco-Excellence campaign."

A Valley Girl straight out of central casting, Marcy stood nearly 6 feet, was skinny as a stork, and had long blond hair worn swept back from her face. Her flat nose, sloped forehead, and small, snakelike lips gave her a slightly elfin look. Many of my colleagues found her attractive; I did not. She personified the corporate handmaiden, taking on characteristics approved by others for her assimilation. She was a hodgepodge of personas created for the satisfaction of those in a position to judge her. I clearly held a minority opinion. Most everyone else bought her shtick.

"You'll recall that our goal by year end is to implement a priority list of office energy-efficiency enhancements. 'The triple Es,' as I call it. But before going further, I want to underscore how proud

I am to be working at a company with a genuine commitment to being green."

I could tell her pep talk was falling flat. Everyone sat lifelessly, staring ahead like corporate automatons downloading the day's marching orders. Perhaps Marcy's excessive toadying inspired the milquetoast response. Or maybe her audience was too preoccupied with its job security, given the lousy economic climate. Mortimer, for his part, smiled broadly at Marcy.

"As I was saying," Marcy went on, her voice reaching a crescendo, "this week we are going to formally launch the Eco-Excellence campaign. It's spring, everyone, so let's spring our consciousness forward."

I suppressed a groan.

"To support the rollout, we have had a steering committee compile a list of office-greening best practices. I have personally overseen its development, along with Shirley Wasserman from HR and Colin McElroy from Econ.

"Of course, this couldn't have been done without Mortimer's leadership." Her outstretched hand swept dramatically in Mortimer's direction, like Adam reaching out to God in the Sistine Chapel. "Everyone will receive an email outlining the action items that all of you, I hope, will take. During our Monday morning meetings, we'll discuss roses and thorns." She beamed at her witty reference, hoping everyone had understood. "Any questions?"

The room was silent.

"Okay," she proceeded undeterred, "you will all soon receive the first set of tasks, but let me take a moment to reveal a few of them here." Though difficult to believe possible, her saccharine enthusiasm reached new heights as she prepared to speak. Then, in a flash, her expression became quite serious.

"Deforestation. Each of you will be asked to purchase and keep by your workstation a potted plant to combat deforestation. Any type will do, provided it's not too large." She was starting to smile again. She just couldn't help herself. "We must not forget the importance of plant life, one of our most important carbon sinks. As you all certainly learned in school, plants consume carbon dioxide and release oxygen. Let's symbolically offset some of our own greenhouse gas emissions right here in the office. Studies have shown such exercises change behavior. Paper usage in offices that have deployed these types of programs has gone down by as much as 40 percent. That's real progress, people!"

Marcy was something of a shape shifter. She did not earnestly live in any of her emotions. Each merely was deployed for opportunistic proposes. The transitions from one to another could be instantaneous, telegraphing her insincerity for all to see, though somehow few did. Her persona had fueled her professional ascent. Not that she lacked smarts—she wasn't dumb. Hardly. But it was cunning, above all, that had put her on the fast track. Such were the corporate game's twisted rules. The shameless thrived.

"Next, we're going to place bins in each corner of the office where used clothes can be deposited. I hope you will all contribute so that your hand-me-downs can be a hand up for someone in need.

"This isn't just about charity. Clothes production, from the irrigation and farming of cotton to the manufacturing and distribution of finished textiles, is carbon intense. Saving a Tee effectively saves a tree!"

I slumped in my chair. Marcy was so pleased with herself. It was nauseating.

"Finally," she said, taking a deep breath and composing herself, "we are initiating what I call 'Tofu Tuesdays.'"

I scanned my colleagues' faces for signs of disbelief. The hypnotic Monday morning haze in the room made their thoughts unreadable. Perhaps the absurd had become the norm. The whole program smelled of yet another vapid, feel-good corporate mandate designed to grab some low-hanging publicity. As usual, the message of substance and positive change was a sham.

"You got it—no meat on those days. It's 100 percent voluntary, of course, but I hope everyone will participate. This exercise also is aimed at raising consciousness, as raising poultry and livestock is far more environmentally taxing than harvesting vegetables.

"More information about all this will be distributed in the days ahead. Let me repeat, this is completely voluntary, but I hope the carnivores in the room will strongly consider taking part. It is, after all, just one meal a week. Abstain so we can sustain!"

Marcy once again thanked Mortimer for his support. He instantly returned the gratitude, complimenting her hard work and dedication. "Marcy, one question, if I may: What would you like us to do with the plants besides water them?"

Marcy replied with the zeal of the true believer, uttering some blather about conscious building that I tuned out. Apathy was the healthy reaction. Yet, I couldn't help but care—not because Marcy had said anything meaningful, but because I spent the majority of my waking hours in her vicinity. She was a reminder of my professional subjugation, of my dependence on the whimsy of my managers.

The deference paid to Marcy by my colleagues galled me.

They actually bought her shit—even Mortimer, who had briefly headed the company's London headquarters. He should have known better. Tall and wiry, Mortimer, a Brit, was in his 50s. He had a narrow, sharp nose on the end of which precariously sat a pair of rectangular bifocals that he habitually peered over, even when reading. His salt-and-pepper hair was kept in place with strict discipline by a small comb he kept in his breast pocket. He never took off his jacket. His dark, pin-striped Italian suits were worn with starched shirts clamped shut at the sleeves with cuff links that clattered loudly on tabletops when he gesticulated.

As a young man, Mortimer had joined the British Foreign Office out of Cambridge, ascended quickly, and after 20 years of distinguished service, cashed in and gone corporate. Falsely modest most of the time, he once announced—to the bafflement of his American subordinates—that he was "middle-lower-upper-class."

The murkiness of class distinctions on this side of the Atlantic irritated Mortimer. Lost without such signposts, he would frequently interject academic, background or pedigree inquiries into his conversations. Like a Rosetta Stone, they helped him decipher the otherwise inscrutable hieroglyphics of class divisions in a country that professed not to have them, but of course did.

Once he surmised the rank of his target, he or she would be put into a neat category. Aristocrats, or close approximations thereof, were embraced as fellow travelers in the land of the unwashed. The rest were treated with complete and utter indifference.

"Marcy," said Angela, a secretary sitting to my left. "I'm allergic to pollen. Every spring, just after the flowers have bloomed, I get feverish and headachy. I can limit my symptoms, if stay away from the park. Dozens of flowing plants in the office might be difficult for me."

"Thank you for the question or, uh, comment, Angela," Marcy replied. "The steering committee has this under control. We consulted an allergist, who said that pollen counts are most concentrated in flowering plants. This is why we'd urge you to get nonflowering varieties. I should have made this clear, though it's all laid out in the guidance you'll be receiving."

"Very thorough," Mortimer added. "Perhaps, Angela, you can speak to Marcy directly after the meeting about any lingering concerns. We are fully committed to the Eco-Excellence campaign, but naturally it cannot come at the expense of anyone's health.

"My own experience as an amateur gardener is that one can mitigate exposure to pollen with common sense. That can mean staying indoors when pollen counts are high and choosing plants, as Marcy said, that do not flower. Still, let's approach this with caution. If Angela and others have adverse reactions, we'll have to rethink things."

He looked across the room for Angela's approval, receiving it in the form of a nod. It was one of the few times he had actually recognized her as a sentient human being rather than a commoner whom he avoided. Mortimer's estimation of me did not differ greatly. His initial interest and doting—I suspect because my name potentially implied a distinguished Anglo-Saxon pedigree—waned when he eventually learned by happenstance of my parents' relatively humble station in life.

My organizational descent coincided with Marcy's ascent. She had joined Marshland Cooper a few months after me. Initially, Mortimer treated her with cordial detachment until she mentioned that her father, a prominent real estate developer in Los Angeles, was an acquaintance of California's governor. Curiosity piqued, Mortimer probed and Marcy happily obliged. He perked up when she shared that her father knew many elected officials. "How interesting, Marcy." Sensing an opportunity, she dished out a full half hour of details about her illustrious father and his many notable friends.

Within several months, she was promoted. Shortly thereafter, a second promotion. As she ascended, Marcy's confidence grew, along with guile that belied her airhead veneer. While she had deployed her charm with equanimity when first joining the firm, success led to a more discriminating stance. She parceled out her attention like a precious resource. Soon, only those above her in the pecking order received attention—a classic manage up, not down, strategy.

While the Marcy spectacle was demoralizing, my morale was already in a death spiral. I had joined Marshland Cooper after a stint in Washington at the Treasury Department, where economic analysis on energy policy was my specialization following graduate school. While I'd enjoyed the job for a while, I eventually grew tired of it, along with Washington, a one-industry town full of one-dimensional people. New York beckoned. The time was right. I made for greener pastures. Fortune favors the bold. Well, not always.

Marshland Cooper served a niche. Founded by a hotshot policy wonk who'd made a name for himself in the British government, the firm provided political risk analyses about market conditions in politically unstable places. Headquartered in London, it had offices in Hong Kong, Pretoria, and New York. The firm had grown quickly, nearly doubling in size during my three-year tenure. It also had a growing media profile. Senior executives often appeared as talking heads on television, analyzing the market impact of natural disasters, political upheavals, and acts of terror. "Grim is Good, Good is Grim" was the firm's unofficial motto. On several occasions, after returning home from an especially long day, I'd turn on the television only to hear Mortimer droning on about some looming catastrophe.

Following a number of additional mind-numbing announcements, the morning meeting mercifully came to close an hour after it began. As everyone began to disperse, Mortimer hailed me and two other colleagues and asked us to stay behind.

"Sorry for the bother, but I wanted to briefly discuss the MalayNG account. It won't take long. Brad, if I may," he said when the room cleared, "how are the tables coming?"

Brilliant Brad, as he was known around the office, nervously leafed through a stack of papers and fidgeted with his round spectacles. A dry-witted savant and the office's dazzlingly bright number cruncher, Brad had thin lips and nose and two piercing brown eyes that suggested keen powers of observation. With remarkable ease, he turned out truly artful tables and graphs highlighting complex data. If Brilliant Brad presented a graph, it told an elegant story every bit as accessible as he was not.

"Yes, Mortimer." Brad nervously pulled out several multicolored tables and charts from his stack. "I put these together on energy consumption in Chhattisgarh and Orissa," referring to two politically unstable states in India. He pushed the papers across the table to Mortimer, who peered over his bifocals to examine them. His cuff links tapped out an irregular beat as they clinked on the table while he leafed through the document.

"I see," Mortimer murmured, pausing. "Well done, Brad. But perhaps this one should have a different color scheme. And the pie wedges in this chart showing potential megawatt output don't stand out. They're a bit of a jumble. Please rectify. Also, can we do some bar graphs as well? Perhaps a basic one on per-capita energy consumption or the number of attacks in the states. Yes, that would do the trick. Nothing too elaborate.

"We also need to lay out what MalayNG's competitors are doing in the region. It would be very useful if we could represent it schematically by monetary investment. Another on total FDI also would be valuable."

Brilliant Brad nodded and Mortimer motioned to me. "Liv, how is the backgrounder? Have you managed to get current intelligence that we can feed into the piece ahead of our meeting?"

I replied that I had spoken with a journalist from India and a few academics, and that I had a meeting with the Indian consulate later in the week and another with an energy expert early the following week. "I'll have a draft for you soon," I said, "perhaps by the close of business next Friday."

Mortimer nodded approvingly. "Excellent. But don't get stuck in the weeds. We're not trying to write a long-winded dissertation on the insurgency. No value-add there. We want to focus on the prospects going forward: Does the insurgency have legs? What are the national and state governments doing to combat it? Are other investors shunning the region? Those sorts of questions—about two-thousand words total."

I nodded.

Mortimer then turned to Michael, an energy guru who'd joined Marshland Cooper after twenty years of government service. A frumpy man in his fifties with a double chin, potbelly, and unruly wisps of hair that lawlessly protruded in every direction from his balding crown, Michael looked like a weathered bureaucrat. His mind, though, was everything his appearance was not.

We called him "the Rainmaker" around the office—his expertise often cited in the firm's marketing.

"Michael, have you spoken with Dr. Ibrahim recently?" Mortimer inquired, referring to the head of the American subsidiary MalayNG, the Malaysian energy concern that had contracted Marshland Cooper to perform an analysis of India's restive states.

Michael replied he would be having a conference call tomorrow with several contacts from the firm before the face-to-face meeting with MalayNG's senior management the following month in San Francisco.

"Brilliant," Mortimer said. "Which brings me to that meeting. I know you're the lead on this, Michael. But we're trying to keep overhead costs down right now in light of the tough economic climate. We might need to pare down the team heading out west. It's not finalized yet, of course, but it might just be Marcy and me on this occasion."

Michael's eyes widened. "But Mortimer," he protested, "I've been in close contact with Dr. Ibrahim for over a year now. I'm our primary contact for MalayNG. It would look, quite frankly, unprofessional not to have the account lead at the meeting. We'd seem out of our depth. Our message would be diluted. Besides, nobody knows more about India's energy sector than me."

Mortimer tried to calm Michael. "I argued your case to Oliver," he explained, referring to Marshland Cooper's managing director. "The problem is, revenues are down three percent this quarter and five for the year. The recession is cutting deep. We just can't afford to take a full complement."

I suspected there was more to it. Marcy, seeking to monopolize Mortimer's attention, may have persuaded him to take her and no one else by tapping into her family network. Perhaps she had even arranged through her father an introduction to the governor in Sacramento. The inducement would be impossible for Mortimer to resist; he was as enthralled by proximity to power as he was to pedigree. He'd leap at the opportunity.

"We may be short of cash," Michael retorted, "but we don't want to shoot ourselves in the foot by undermining one of our best revenue streams. MalayNG is a cash cow."

"Agreed," Mortimer nodded. "We're being penny wise, pound foolish. It's not my call, though. Oliver is firm on this. He also wants us to start flying coach. Of course, I objected vigorously... but it was no use. I'm afraid we're in for a period of austerity."

Michael continued pleading his case, all the while recognizing its futility. "Very well, then," Mortimer said, breaking the awkward silence that followed. "I suggest you reach out to Dr. Ibrahim in the days ahead so that he can ask any technical questions he has ahead of our meeting. Also, you and I should get together to discuss the account, so I'll be fully prepared. Maybe you could also draw up a brief I can use.

"And since Marcy will be there, on account of her being the lead on the call on Ambertson & Phillips in Oakland, maybe we can try to exploit her talents by carving out a role for her. For example, she could update MalayNG on the competitive marketplace. Sound good? Okay, then, that's it. Fingers crossed, the meeting won't go pear shaped."

Michael briskly retrieved his papers and marched out of the conference room with Brilliant Brad close behind. On my way back to my office, I crossed paths in the hallway with Cory, a recently hired twenty-something with a tart sense of humor.

"So what plant are you going to get?" I asked him. "Me, I'm

leaning toward a cactus. Or maybe a Venus flytrap—that would be an apt metaphor for this place."

"You're such a schemer," Cory replied dryly, giving me a slap on the shoulder. "I'll bet you have a whole assortment of tricks up your sleeve."

I retreated to my workspace and checked my in-box again. A message from Alex proposed dinner the following day. A close friend, Alex worked for a prominent financial institution that nearly brought down the global economy. I arranged to meet Alex at a trendy French restaurant on the Upper East Side.

The rest of my workday unfolded uneventfully, though Michael did visit my cubicle to complain bitterly. I tread carefully. Michael had a reputation for loose lips. "This place is insane," he huffed. I identified. The place was nuts. His getting shut out of a business trip probably had something to do with Marcy. But I did not want to risk my sentiments about her or any aspect of the firm becoming public on account of Michael's gossiping, so I merely nodded modestly. He trotted off in search of a more sympathetic audience.

As soon as work was over, I made for the elevator and practically ran through marble lobby out into the torrential downpour. In such weather, the rare cabs became prized commodities, prompting a frenzy when an unoccupied one appeared. The veneer of civilization was violently exposed on these sorts of days. Waterlogged New Yorkers were not to be crossed as they jockeyed for positions in greedy anticipation.

Seeing the long line and without any viable ride-hailing options, I pulled my raincoat up over my head and walked toward the subway. At the end of the block, I crossed at the light and walked several more blocks through the crush of soaked pedestrians. I turned the corner at Madison and came face-to-face with a group of Comitans.

Even in this miserable weather, they were out, defiant and snide. Their clothes were wet, their placards soggy. The markers used to write livid phrases had run, leaving inky lines of residue, as if oil-soaked snails had slithered down them. Undeterred, they seethed and shouted.

I waded through the thicket and ducked into the subway, my sanctuary for the moment.

LOVABLE ROGUE

The Patriot Posse, a collection of reactionary lunatics and misfits, held a convention in Dallas during which its founder, a popular right-wing radio personality, Edward Schmidt, warned the self-styled defenders of liberty of "world government" and "collectivism." He closed by repeating "Posse Comitatus," a reference to the Posse Comitatus Act, a post-Reconstruction law limiting the government's ability to deploy armed forces domestically for law enforcement. The crowd rose to its feet in restless euphoria, echoing the invocation and giving birth to the Comitans movement.

The otherwise boilerplate, paranoid, right-wing tirade probably would have faded away were it not for the stock market plunging twelve percent six months later. When the country's second-largest financial institution confirmed it was overleveraged in Latin America, a bank run ensued. Within days, two other banks failed. By week's end, markets in Europe and Asia had collapsed. So began a calamity born from a bubble relating to real estate in places like Argentina. It was said that at the speculative peak, land in the Buenos Aires slums was priced on par with top locations in New York and London.

The president, the scion of a prominent family and in over his head, tried to restore calm with a nationally televised address. "The business cycle has reasserted itself," he said calmly. "We've been here before, and we're going to be here again. The key is to not panic." Panic ensued.

The stock market plummeted another five percent the next day. Minutes after the closing bell, a banker shot himself in front of his colleagues. Another jumped to his death from the Brooklyn Bridge. "Again?" one national newspaper's headline asked on its front page, which sported a Depression-era photo of a breadline.

In frightening succession, America's largest companies announced massive layoffs. A famous retail chain filed for bankruptcy, as did the nation's biggest automotive-parts manufacturer. Consumer confidence plummeted.

Congress took emergency action by cutting taxes and appropriating billions of dollars in infrastructure spending. The Central Bank lowered interest rates and bailed out Wall Street.

Yet the bleeding continued.

Two-hundred-thousand Comitans from around the country, menaced by humiliation both real and imagined, converged on Washington, DC, on the anniversary of the Posse Comitatus Act's enactment, just as the crisis was intensifying. Schmidt addressed the angry protestors. Many carried flags with the movement's yellow standard featuring an eagle with a snake in its beak, below which read *Aut consiliis aut ense*"—"*By counsel or by the sword.*"

Schmidt cited the usual suspects—the media, financiers, liberals, Muslims, and so on—seeking to overturn the Constitution and rule by fiat. "Our precious nation has never faced such danger," he yelled, banging his fist on the podium. "Never. At the dawn of our country's founding, great men like Franklin, Madison, and Washington bravely fought to ensure that this proud nation, under God, would never perish from this earth. Not then, not now!" As the crowd shouted its approval, he thundered, "Demonstrate. Demonstrate. Demonstrate. As long as we have that right, demonstrate. And when we don't, we'll demonstrate our displeasure in a very different way."

Schmidt was an unlikely skipper of this particular ship. Before rising to national prominence as a right-wing blowhard, he'd hawked homeopathic cures for terminal illnesses and End Times survival guides. He had declared bankruptcy six times and even settled a multimillion-dollar insurance fraud suit, narrowly avoiding prison. His personal life was similarly seedy. Married multiple times, each time to ever more voluptuous models, Schmidt repeatedly had been sued for sexual assault, including by an underage intern. He'd settled out of court on each occasion.

Like a sleazy swindler, as depicted on cable television, the hefty sixty-six-year-old sported a pompadour of dubious authenticity and vibrant golden sheen that, like New England autumn foliage, changed daily. His perma-tan completed the look, giving him a pumpkin polish, except around his eyes, presumably where he wore protective goggles when bronzing. "I'm fuckin' gorgeous," he volunteered once, "and hung like Sasquatch."

None of this diminished his support among the converted, including evangelicals who supposedly championed "family values." Nothing, it seemed, could damper their fervor for him. His was a cult of personality. As such, at Schmidt's urging, civil disobedience spread. Comitans staged sit-ins in cities and towns alike. Even an IHOP outside Denver was overrun by the belligerent malcontents, who refused to vacate the premises until all "collectivists" and "progressives" left or, failing that, relinquished their trays of assorted maple syrups.

I, like many others, dismissed the Comitans at first. There was something buffoonish about them. They comprised a veritable self-parody of unhinged reactionaries, with their false nostalgia about an imagined past and an apocalyptic present. And who could take their leader seriously...until they arrived in Manhattan?

For the second time in almost as many days, a Comitan accosted me, this time as I exited the subway. He was wearing a hat emblazoned with an American flag, under which read the motto "I love my country but fear its leaders." I tried to ignore him, but he persisted. "Hey, you!" he growled. "You—yes, you, dirty bastard!" I elbowed my way through the thicket of people, crossing Third Avenue. "The reckoning is coming," he yelled after me.

I hurried off, but the rush-hour crush was at its peak. The rain-soaked sidewalk was dark and slippery like wet linoleum and smelled of moist cardboard. The city was pulsing with barely contained chaos, a steam engine running at full tilt, its pistons violently thrusting up and down.

While I was negotiating the gauntlet, a hand grabbed my arm, pulling me toward the corner of the block. I staggered to maintain my balance, surprised by the strength and resolve of my unseen captor.

"You!" another Comitan sneered. He was enormous, standing a full head taller than me and wearing a long trench coat, black boots, and baseball cap with a patch that read "Freedom." His long, narrow face had a twisted scar running down one unshaven cheek. A tattoo of an American flag fluttering in the breeze adorned his reptilian neck. His dark, hooded eyes squinted at me and I recoiled.

"You," he snarled again, still holding my arm. "I saw you pull down my buddy's poster a block back, outside the subway. Don't deny it."

"What are you talking about?" I shot back, yanking my arm from his grasp. "Get the fuck off me."

"Don't deny it," he repeated. "I saw you. Have the courage of your convictions."

"I have no idea what you're talking about. I didn't rip down anyone's poster. I don't do that sort of thing. I respect free speech. Not like you and your fascist buddies."

I stomped off.

"The revolution is coming," the Comitan boomed after me. "It's coming! Just wait. I'm John Galt! *I'm John Galt!*"

Useful idiocy is an American tradition. In the Civil War, countless Confederate soldiers gave their lives to preserve their own impoverishment, since employment in the region's dominant sector, agriculture, furnished by enslaved blacks, was off-limits to them. Thus, a monument to them and their ideological heirs could appropriately reference a famous fictional character whose "heroic" struggle against the undeserving masses stirred many an imagination. It would read, "I am John Galt."

I walked down the streets that, in the relentless downpour, were transformed into small canals crawling with coffee cups, pizza boxes, and the occasional rat. Gondola futures seemed like a good investment in this environment. I managed to hail a cab before being set upon by a waterlogged mob. "Midtown," I said, adding, Les Parisiennes, referencing the French restaurant that was all the rage despite the recession—or maybe because of it.

New York eateries, like all fashionable commodities, have mysterious life cycles. For no apparent reason, one becomes an overnight sensation while another shutters its doors. What they lack in culinary quality they make up for in lavish explanations for what is on offer, along with garish interior designs.

The cabbie groaned when I mentioned my destination. "Again? You must be the fourth person this week. I've never heard of the place before. I'll bet it won't be around next year. Always works that way. Here today, gone tomorrow."

The rain had tapered off by the time we arrived at the restaurant, though not enough to preclude a fight for the cab. Two women in smart business attire shot forward as the vehicle pulled up to the curb. Both jockeyed for a position like basketball forwards angling for a rebound. When I poked my head out, they elbowed each other, shouting epithets.

"I was here first, bitch."

"Was not," the other protested before managing to grab her rival's handbag and throwing it down on the sidewalk. Then she slid into the taxi and slammed the door as I exited.

A line of well-dressed guests, perhaps twenty in total, stretched down the block, a sea of protective umbrellas in front of Les Parisiennes. Two concierges, outfitted with radios tucked discreetly inside their suits like Secret Service agents, were stationed at the entrance. Occasionally, one would raise his sleeve to his mouth and mutter into a hidden microphone. It added to the air of exclusivity.

I volunteered my name to the shorter one. "I'm meeting a friend, Alex Cunningham, who has a reservation. He might be here already."

The concierge motioned me forward. A cacophony of voices

and clanging of wine glasses and utensils greeted me as I entered. To my left was a neon-lit bar manned by several beret-wearing bartenders busily pouring drinks. Stylish patrons sat on a line of leather stools; a vacant one was monogrammed with the Eiffel Tower.

"Mr. Ackerman?" asked a pretty brunette wearing a shapely business suit.

"Yes, that's me."

"Mr. Cunningham is waiting. This way, *s'il vous plaît*." She flashed a flirtatious smile and pointed me in the direction of the dining room, a forest of white-linen-adorned tables where dozens of well-heeled guests sat dressed to the nines.

Waiters in black ties carrying trays stacked with silver-dish-covered plates moved about with the practiced precision of theater stagehands. An elaborate chandelier hung from a ceiling decorated with a faux fresco. The scene featured a woman in a tunic stretching a beefy arm out to grasp a glass of wine offered up by a male suitor in armor, behind which scores of revelers were enjoying the bacchanal. It was a grotesque counterpoint to the economic malaise gripping the country. Perhaps that was the point.

"Monsieur, did you get struck in the rain?" the *maître d'* asked.

"Not really," I responded.

"*Très bien*. The city can be very difficult to navigate on days like today. But you're here, which is all that matters."

The *maître d'* shepherded me through the dining room to a table in the far corner where Alex was sitting. He was on the phone. Motioning apologetically for me to sit down, he whispered, "I'll be off in a sec. It's my boss."

Alex, blond and blue-eyed, had a button nose, square jaw, and two rows of perfectly aligned teeth. Muscular yet sinewy, he stood six-foot-two and sported two extravagantly long arms that were in perpetual motion. He carried himself with a casual indifference easily mistaken for arrogance.

The son of two left-wing academics, Alex had grown up in Southern California. With the benefit of his massive wingspan for balance, he became such an accomplished surfer that he contemplated delaying college to compete professionally. He was also a math genius. In elementary school, he'd wowed teachers with a complex equation that attempted to explain wave action. By high school, he was taking college-level classes. NASA recruited him out of high school, but he chose MIT instead and graduated in three years.

Like many graduates of America's most prestigious schools, Alex had gravitated toward finance, a profession that, at least superficially, was ill-suited for his devil-may-care deportment and liberal pedigree. And he worked for one of the most prominent Wall Street banks, a notoriously crooked practitioner that was a major contributor to the global financial crisis.

A fast climber in the investment banking division, the bank's heart of darkness, he worked alongside the country's brightest minds and watched them craft financial instruments designed to confuse government regulators. It worked. The Rube Goldberg-like instruments were so complex that nobody understood them. Nobody cared. Why would they? No reason existed for second-guessing as long as the economy was humming along. But then the music stopped.

"It's just a job. That's all," Alex had announced with characteristic cheer when we'd first met three years ago at a Midtown party for a mutual friend. "Some people cut hair, others fix cars. I rip off pensions." It was a joke, of course. Or was it? At the time, I wondered.

"Yeah, I know," he said into the phone, now speaking loudly over the restaurant's din, while I took in the gaudy décor. "I'm gonna get on that later. They're overleveraged and highly geared. They can't afford additional obligations, much less more risk. Their value horizon is real long. Too long. We've got the better hand. It's not even close. I'm going do a few more go-rounds with different base assumptions, but I think we're solid. We…right… right. Okay, I'll do it. Yeah. Okay. Bye."

I bided my time by scanning the surroundings. The dining room was filled to capacity. The patrons tended to be middle-aged, with a few exceptions, and all were formally attired. I did not see a black face among them. New York was among the world's most diverse cities, a glorious melting pot. But you wouldn't have known that here. Les Parisiennes might as well have been in Wyoming.

Alex hung up and leaned over the table to give me a hug, enveloping me with his gangly arms. "Dude," he said in true Californian fashion, "I didn't think you were going to make it. I thought you might have been washed away. It's crazy out there."

"Yeah, God's angry at Wall Street, so he decided it's time to start over. I'm building an ark."

"Nope. Not true. We would've been flooded out decades ago if that were so."

"God's behind schedule," I replied.

"Oh, in that case, can I get a spot?"

"On the ark? You'll have to sit next to a pair of goats and two llamas."

"That's fine. Compared to my asshole boss, I can handle anything. I'm special," he added in jest.

I rolled my eyes. "Yeah, right. You investment bankers are a cut above the rest. Putting that freakish intelligence to use by destroying the world economy."

Alex chuckled and shrugged. "It's a tough job—"

"—but somebody's got to do it," I interjected.

"So, really, did you have any trouble getting here?"

"Not at all," I glanced at the contents of a passing waiter's tray. "I did almost get into a fight with a Comitan, though."

"You serious?"

"One of them confronted me on Third Avenue...accused me of tearing down one of his buddy's posters and looked ready to punch me—"

"*Bienvenue*," a waiter in a dark navy suit interjected in an affected accent that failed to disguise his New Jersey timbre. "I'm Vito." Handing us both menus, he announced the specials, a barrage of culinary claptrap featuring words like "curated" and "infused." He asked for our drink order, but we deferred.

"I thought we'd be spared *them*," Alex remarked, once the waiter disappeared.

"Waiters speaking French with Jersey Shore accents, you mean?" I laughed.

"No, Comitans. I'd thought they'd stick to Mississippi and Georgia. Now they're here."

"I thought so, too. Then again, the crisis started here." I coughed dramatically, indicting Alex.

"I know you think that I personally brought down the global economy, Liv, but you're wrong. I didn't. I had the help of many, many colleagues."

We both laughed.

"Strange," Alex continued, "how the people getting most screwed are supporting those doing most of the screwing—the politicians cutting social programs while lining the pockets of—"

"People like you," I said, pouncing.

"Yeah, exactly, people like me. 'Thank you, sir, may I have another?' Explain that to me."

"That sort of populism always blames one sinister group or another—the media, some minority, liberals, and so on—for fucking over *real* Americans. They ignore the true culprits by design. It never fails. What's that saying? 'There are no second acts in American lives.' Wrong. Bigots never go out of style."

"That's harsh stuff," Alex observed. "Why didn't you tell that to the Comitan who accosted you? I'm sure he would've appreciated it."

"Right," I replied sharply. "They're total bullshit. They complain about government tyranny, but they tyrannize everyone in their orbit. Just imagine if their types actually had serious power. Scary.

"Regardless, we wouldn't even be having this discussion were it not for you yahoos in finance responsible for this shitshow. The Comitans are your creation. If it wasn't for the financial crisis, they'd be a local problem, not a national menace."

"Look, I'll take my lumps," Alex admitted, holding up his palms. "We fucked up. But that's what we do. We fuck up. We're in the wealth-creation business. And by 'we' I mean all of Wall Street, and by 'wealth creation,' I mean for us. We enrich ourselves at others' expense."

I did not know if Alex sincerely meant what he was saying or just trying to egg me on. He could be hard to read. "How do you do it? I mean, how do you do what you do, knowing that what you're doing is total bullshit. It's dangerous bullshit that causes so much harm."

"Ah, Liv," Alex answered, waving me away playfully, "all jobs are bullshit. That's the definition of a job: a consuming activity, typically done in a location outside one's residence, that has no purpose or social benefit."

"You really believe that?"

"Don't you?"

"Well..."

"You should by now," Alex said before I could finish my thought. "I figured it out years ago. I recall the exact moment. It was in business school. In my second year, I had a class with a cranky old Marxist. Why he was teaching at the place was unclear. He did not fit in. He even wore tweed suits—you know, the ones with the elbow patches. He was practically a caricature of an academic.

"One day, he began lecturing about this economist. I forget his name. In the 1930s, this economist had predicted that, based on productivity growth, people would have to work only fifteen hours a week in the not-too-distant future. That's all that would be necessary. At that point, the class laughed. But here's the rub: it actually happened. Not the limited hours—we work more today than ever. But productivity rates did increase as predicted."

"So?" I asked.

"So, here's the sixty-four-thousand-dollar question: we're productive enough to only work minimal hours in order to provide for our basic needs, but we don't. Why not? That was the professor's question."

"Well," I responded, "maybe because we don't work just to

afford food, shelter, and other necessities. We want more, and we work accordingly."

"That's definitely part of it. A few people in class made that very point. But the professor reminded us that if we're working more than half of the week to pay for those consumer goods and luxuries, then the industrial sector involved in furnishing those same goods and luxuries should dominate the economy. But it doesn't."

I had lost the thread, and I was getting hungry. "Okay, what's your point?"

"My point is," Alex said, leaning in close, "I understood at that very moment what the old Marxist was implying. I got it."

"That we really don't have to work as many hours as we do?"

"Yes, but more importantly, that most jobs don't have any real purpose or function. They're not needed. They're there simply to be there."

"Like your job, Alex?"

"Yeah, like mine, but not just mine. Armies of paper pushers—mid-level managers, lawyers, accountants, administrators, bankers, bureaucrats, consultants, and so on—exist purely to exist. Think about it. How many people do you know that have genuinely useful jobs, jobs that would truly be missed if they didn't show up for work? A handful at best.

"The irony is that genuinely useful jobs tend not to pay and lack prestige. Very few people would actually be missed. A caretaker for the elderly? Yes. A social worker? Absolutely. An elementary school teacher? No doubt. Firefighter of policeman? Damn straight.

"However, the most important 'job' of all—raising children—pays squat! The relationship between socially useful and socially useless work is inverse. That's why I went into finance. I figured I might as well find a top-paying bullshit job, so I could make a killing and get out of the game as quickly as possible. I have no aptitude for non-bullshit jobs."

Vito returned.

"*Bonjour, messieurs.* Have you decided if you'd like to order off our wine menu?"

"Yes," Alex said confidently, glancing at the list. "We'll share a bottle of Bordeaux. How 'bout…" Alex paused, scanning the options. "The Château Marquis de Savoyard, 1989."

"A fine choice, *monsieur.* I'll bring it right over."

"The Château Marquis de Sade?" I asked. "Sounds lethal."

"Yes," Alex replied with a wicked smile, "a fine vintage."

"When did you become a frickin' sommelier?"

"I'm not. I pick by price."

"Great," I sighed. "And how much is the Marquis de Sade going to set us back?"

"Don't worry, I'll expense it. Your meal, too—it's on me…on the bank, that is."

"Or on me, really, given that your employer requires regular bailouts from taxpayers like me. But why fret the details? So," I inquired, "how do you spend most of your waking hours doing something you know is meaningless?"

"Well, first let's be honest here. In most places of the world at most times in history, including now, people didn't have the luxury to ask such questions. Those 'does-my-life-having-meaning?' ones have a name: white man's problems."

"Fine," I sighed. I was getting annoyed. "But how do you do your particular bullshit job in good conscience?"

"Like I said, I personally don't do crazy shit. I help my clients raise money in capital markets. That's the simple version. Nothing rotten. The sketchy shit goes on elsewhere in the building."

I decided not to push the matter further. Alex had a dark sense of humor about his work. But even he might have his limits, which I did not want to test. "So how's your job going?" I asked, my tone changing from accusatory to investigatory.

"Same old, same old."

"Same old hours?"

"Yeah, give or take. I've gotta head back to work after dinner. I've got to finish a presentation."

"I thought your hours would be reduced as you moved up the ladder. No more eighty-hour-plus weeks."

"That's how it works—in theory, at least. The reality is different. It's driven by the corporate culture. You know how it is. You work in Manhattan, too."

I did know, but I wanted to hear it from him anyway. It felt good to hear about the rat race from another rodent running the gauntlet. There was comfort knowing you weren't alone. "Tell me," I said.

Alex sighed. "It's simple. You work hard initially to make a good impression and, more importantly, because it's expected. You've got to prove you're a gunner. That's everywhere, probably, but even more so in such a competitive environment. 'Low performers,' including those unwilling to turn over their entire life to the job, are fired regularly.

"You think things will change once you achieve the next step—senior associate, management, executive, board, et cetera—but it never does. You may advance in absolute terms, but you won't in relative terms. It's a form of keeping up with the Joneses.

"Besides, as you rise, the competition stiffens, so in some ways you're not really getting ahead as much as getting ahead of those that aren't getting ahead. You're effectively standing still. It's a treadmill, Liv, a well-paid treadmill."

"Why don't you get off the treadmill?" Again, I knew the answer, but wanted to hear it from Alex.

"That's the plan." Alex took a sip of water. "For now, though, I'm just trying to survive this economic crisis."

"What crisis? You guys are thriving."

The waiter reappeared holding a white-linen-draped wine bottle, which he presented to Alex. "*Monsieur*," he said. Alex peered at the bottle and nodded. The waiter then produced a corkscrew and, with a few rigorous twists, opened the bottle and gently poured several thimblefuls into Alex's wineglass.

Alex peered into the vessel, placed it beneath his nose, and gave it a gentle swirl. Once it was sufficiently aerated, he took a sip. He squinted and tipped his head back, as if in deep contemplation. A second nod prompted the waiter to pour the vintage into our respective wineglasses. He then placed the cork on the table.

"Do you gentlemen know what you'd like to order tonight?"

"I think we'll need a bit more time," Alex responded. "My friend here thinks this is an interview."

The waiter bowed and departed.

"What the hell was that, Alex?"

"What?"

"What do you mean, what? That ridiculous display with the wine!"

"Don't hate me because I'm sophisticated," Alex feigned disappointment.

"Seriously, Alex, what do you know about wine? Would you know the difference if it was Manischewitz?"

"Ah, the wine of God's whiniest people," Alex shot back playfully, aware of my own Jewish heritage. "Why would I want to drink Jewish wine after hours? I have to work with *your people* all day as it is! Finance is controlled by Jews!"

"Oh, you didn't," I responded with mock indignation. "I didn't realize you'd become a Comitan!"

Alex exploded in hilarity.

"So what's the plan?" I asked.

"You mean my life plan? That's a big question."

"When are you getting off the treadmill?"

"Well, like I said, I want to put in another five or ten years. By then, I'll have enough to head back out west."

"And do what?"

"Surf. Open a beach bar. Smoke weed. I don't know. Not work, mainly—no more commuting, no more long hours, no more office politics, no more bullshit."

"That sounds reasonable. Isn't that everyone's dream in your line of work? But nobody actually leaves when they have 'enough.' More likely, they die of a coronary at their desk...at fifty-five...long after their bank accounts have added lots of zeros."

"True," Alex concurred. "It's a cliché. I guess you get used to the rhythm, the money, and so on. It makes it difficult to leave. You've heard the saying. A frog won't budge in a pot of water brought to a slow boil."

"Maybe." But I was unconvinced. "Or maybe they stay because, oddly, they think they're making a difference."

"Hell, no!" Alex bellowed. "It's about status. Peacocking. And money, of course. Trying to untangle pay from status is like untangling sex from nymphomania. It's practically one and the same. Besides, few make a difference anyway. Remember, it's Bullshit Central."

Vito returned to take our order. Alex politely requested elaboration on several menu items, which clarified little, as every explanation answered the question at hand but raised a host of others.

The Duxelle of Chanterelles was, in fact, a "mélange of mushroom stems, onions, shallots, and herbs sautéed in butter." But tonight the chef had substituted it with a "pâté feuilletée with a rich port and elderberry sauce for the aligot de l'Aubrac." And the "mille-feuille" was synonymous with a Napoleon, but the "coussin de Lyon" that accompanied it remained of mysterious provenance.

We gave up.

Alex ordered the least enigmatic offering, a steak with some vegetable concoction. I did the same.

"So, how's work for you?" Alex asked, finally turning the tables.

I sighed.

"No surprise there," Alex observed tartly. "Like I said, you've got a white man's problem. You could always apply to this place. I understand they need waiters. You just need a shitty French accent and the ability to make up culinary nonsense on the fly."

"Exactly!"

"That's right—when in doubt, just make shit up. 'Oh, sir, the hen McElroy served on a bed of parsnip-ladled shallots and kale is one of my favorites. The hens are free range, reared in Ireland, and massaged daily as they grow to ensure their meat is tender.'"

"But of course," I chimed in, assuming an affected accent.

We doubled over and howled.

"Does the job really stink, Liv?"

"Yeah, it's frustrating." I recounted the latest environmental campaign and Marcy's most recent coup. "I got out of a dead-end public sector job in hopes that I'd find my calling in the private sector. But I'm starting to think that it's all the same. Public or private, big firm or single proprietorship, Fortune 500 or NGO. It's called a job for a reason. But I guess I should be grateful to still have employment, given how many people don't."

Alex nodded knowingly before excusing himself to take a call from a colleague. I fidgeted in a room filled with Manhattan's ruling class, trying to look at ease. When that grew old, I attempted to calculate the amount the restaurant's current patrons would spend on their dinner collectively. My estimate was equivalent to the price of a mid-size sedan. Not a bad haul.

Alex returned ten minutes later.

"Sorry 'bout that," he said. "I've got this client presentation and…oh, well, the truth is that it's always like this. Fuckin' work phone. I'm like a doctor on call. The thing even rings in the middle of the night. And guess what? I answer it!"

"Sounds like a white man's problem to me," I cracked.

Alex laughed. "Yeah," he said, holding his hand aloft, "but here's the difference: I accept my fate, which is easy since I know it's not all that bad. You're constantly fighting it because you think it's really awful when it's not. You need some perspective."

"Agreed. Our ancient ancestors probably weren't too riddled with existential angst," I remarked, "a point you made earlier. Staying alive was their preoccupation. But times have changed— at least for us fortunate few. We have the luxury to be concerned with existential shit. That goes without saying. But given that we're in the position to contemplate life's purpose—and many people do—how is it that we continue doing such pointless work that consumes so much of our lives?"

The question went unanswered as our waiter reappeared at the table, this time carrying two plates covered by silver domes, which he removed, adding "*Voilà!*" for dramatic effect.

The presumed steak, a blackened hockey-puck-sized object, was the only vaguely recognizable offering. A medley of alleged vegetables and purported potatoes created a multicolored tableau garnished with a sprig of parsley.

"Ah, *oui*," I said in a posh French accent once the waiter had departed, "our *je ne sais quoi* looks delicious. A toast."

We both raised our glasses.

"To bullshit jobs."

"To bullshit angst," Alex added.

"And to bullshit restaurants," I parried.

We both sipped our wine. The Marquis de Sade went down smoothly.

CHAPTER 3

PLACEHOLDERS

Gita's number flashed across my phone with an accompanying vibration, giving me a start, as it always did when she rang. The response was induced by eager anticipation, or perhaps skittishness, or both.

I answered.

"Livie, why didn't you call last night? I was so worried. Are you okay?"

"Yes, I'm fine," I replied with indifference, a strategic counterpoint to Gita's typically reproachful air. "I was with Alex."

"Oh," she replied, "you didn't mention that."

I had. Gita had forgotten conveniently or, more likely, pretended to have forgotten my plans, hence her thinly veiled guilt trip, a diversionary tactic likely deployed before a full-frontal assault. She was softening me up for the hammer blow.

Gita's dislike of Alex was genuine, visceral even. Mere mention of his name induced eye rolls, casting an instant pall over any conversation, as if he were a rogue relative whose regular encounters with the law caused great shame. I suspected this was due to a well-founded suspicion that he had her number.

They had met on just two occasions, each time by chance, once at a coffee shop and the other time in Central Park. Alex, lacking any pretension, easily spotted pretense in others, dispelling the notion it takes one to know one. He could recognize that which he was not.

"She's very pretty," he had remarked after their first encounter, which occurred months after she and I began dating. "And obviously accomplished, too. She has much to be proud of—and she is."

Gita always shifted nervously in Alex's presence, perhaps sensing that her charms were lost on him. Her false humility about her budding medical career, which typically endeared her to those with a less finely tuned ear, rang hollow. Alex had smiled politely at her description of medicine as merely "anatomical car mechanics" and her claim that her decision to become a physician was arbitrary and not, as was actually the case, a dogged pursuit for professional preeminence.

Gita told me her aversion to Alex was a matter of principle. She was a conscientious objector of Wall Street. No scoundrel of great wealth could be her friend. Alex was one of *them*, a fabulously compensated mercenary for the fiendish forces of finance, a wrongdoer in pinstripes. "People like him offer nothing. They create nothing. They *are* nothing."

Gita's righteous indignation was transparently dishonest; some of her own friends were in finance. Besides, Alex's profession, whatever its merits, was entirely irrelevant, since Gita was aggressively apolitical. She cared not a whit about the world outside medicine, a viewpoint vindicated, she believed, by the vocation's prestige.

"I was so worried," she claimed implausibly. "I tried reaching you a bunch of times. You didn't notice I'd phoned?"

I had turned off my phone at the restaurant, I explained, prompting her to ask where we had dined.

"Oh, you didn't, Livie," Gita protested. "I have heard such great things about Les Parisiennes! You can make it up to me tonight. Take me there." Her voice trailed off. "I'm done at seven. I'm not working a triple," she added, referencing the occasional thirty-six-hour shifts put in by medical residents, "so I won't be totally shattered. I deserve it. And you owe me for last night."

"Ummm..." I tried to recall whether I had anything else going on. I didn't. But did I really want to go to the same ridiculous restaurant two nights in a row? I had no choice. "Oh, okay, that should work."

"Great," she responded, "make the reservations. Look, I'm sorry, but I can't talk now. I've got to go back to rounds in a few minutes. I just was calling to see if you were okay."

"Oh," I replied, somewhat dazed by the trap I had walked into.

"Meet me in front of Lennox," Gita declared, referring to Lennox Hill Hospital on the Upper East Side, where she was in her second year of residency. "Seven sharp. Don't be late, Livie."

New York was again a soggy mess when I set out to retrieve Gita. The subway entrance was overflowing with drenched commuters seeking refuge from yet another downpour—their task complicated by the presence of a phalanx of churlish Comitans hurling insults at passersby.

To avoid the protestors, as well as the subway itself, a subterranean labyrinth packed with urban refugees, I opted to walk the ten blocks instead. As a consequence of my detour, I arrived at Lennox Hill soaked and 20 minutes late. Gita was waiting impatiently in the foyer.

"Livie, I've been here forever," Gita said. "What took you so long?"

She had changed out of her scrubs and was wearing designer jeans, a form-fitting sweater, and heels. Over her shoulder was slung a large tote bag in which she typically carried the tools of her trade: a white coat, stethoscope, spare scrubs, Crocs™, and several packs of stimulants to stave off sleep.

Despite having just worked twelve hours, she was radiant and gorgeous. About average height and skinny, Gita had coffee skin complemented by flowing dark hair that she tended to wear pulled back in a bun. Her brown, penetrating doe eyes were framed by long lashes. Her nose was small, her lips thin, and her cheekbones and jaw line pronounced.

A bubbly personality and easy smile hastily put strangers at ease, nullifying the typical intimidation induced by her obvious beauty. However, it was, as Alex perceived, a facade beneath which lurked white-hot intensity, drive, and ego.

On this day, Gita was wearing her favorite lavender perfume, the smell of which was particularly pronounced as I gave her a hug. Her embrace was limp, more implied than given, indicating that I would have to earn her affection after being tardy.

"Livie, you know I've been at work all day and night. Why did you keep me waiting?"

"Sorry," I replied in the world-weary tone I frequented adopted around her. "The rain made the subway impossibly crowded, so I had to walk. As you can see," I added, pointing to my suit, "I'm wet."

"Yes, you are," Gita groused, a sign that any plea for sympathy was going to fall on deaf ears. "And we're supposed to have dinner tonight at Les Parisiennes. With you looking like a soggy dog, we might as well eat here in the cafeteria." She pointed in the direction from which wafted the smell of saturated-fat-heavy food, an oddity in a building dedicated to the restoration of health.

"You know how hard I work," she said. "I don't have a regular nine-to-five job like you. I don't see the outside of this hospital for days on end, so my down time is precious. You know that. You act like you don't care, Livie."

I was too tired to push back. Avoid acrimony, a married colleague had once counseled about relationships. Give in. I did just that. "I know, Gee," I replied. "Tonight was important to you…"

"And why didn't you call to tell me you were running late?"

"I tried but…"

"Oh, never mind," she said. "This was going to be such a nice evening for *us*."

"It still will be," I insisted with forced sincerity, annoyed by her emphasizing "us," as our relationship was just a little over a year old and going nowhere interesting. We were fundamentally mismatched.

Not that it mattered. Even were it otherwise, a passionate romance was impossible given Gita's demanding schedule as a physician-in-training and my dissatisfaction about my overall station in life. Thus, we were oddly matched despite being fundamentally mismatched. We were placeholders thriving on low expectations.

"I hope so," Gita uttered. "If it's important to me, it should be important to you.

"Yes, you're right," I answered, eager to ascend above the heavy cloud cover. "So how about this: down the block, if I recall, there's a clothing store. I'll buy a sweater and change out of my wet shirt and sport jacket, and then we'll head to whatever restaurant you want, provided it's not a fancy place with a dress code. Your call. Sound good?"

"What about Les Parisiennes?"

I bit my tongue.

"We had reservations, Livie," she protested. "You're always letting me down. So unreliable."

It had been a tough day at work. Mortimer had moved up the deadline for my backgrounder on India's investment climate, and I had received a few unwelcome reminders about the Eco-Excellence campaign. I just wanted to relax. "I promise, we'll go there—soon. It'll be special. But tonight we'll try something else. Deal?"

"Okay," she replied flatly, unconvinced.

We hurried across the block in the rain and down another into a chain clothing store found on any street corner in any town in America and, increasingly, the world. I purchased a T-shirt and V-neck sweater. We caught a taxi across town, and Gita perked up during the drive, recounting an unusual happening at work.

"Just before finishing up my morning rounds, I checked up on a middle-aged woman admitted the previous night because of alcohol poisoning. The concierge at her luxury building on the West Side had found her passed out in front of the place and called the paramedics. Apparently, this had happened before, so the concierge was not particularly alarmed.

"Are you listening?" Gita snapped as I glanced out the window at a passing police car.

I faced her. "Yes, of course."

"Good. As I was saying, despite all that she'd been through the previous night, she looked very sophisticated. And she was very pretty: blond, blue-eyed, and petite, with large white teeth and a small nose. Had I seen her on the street, I might've mistaken her for an actress or maybe a model, though she was a bit old.

"It was clear when I began questioning her to gauge her condition that she also was highly educated. She spoke in a soft and dignified voice that I could've sworn had a hint of a British accent. 'I do apologize for the inconvenience I've caused,' she said. Can you imagine that, Livie? 'Inconvenience'? She must've gone to an Ivy League school." Gita would know, given her own education at Princeton.

I nodded. I had a feeling that her story was going in a direction that would irritate me. This happened often.

"Strangely, though, nobody had visited her since her admission the night before. Not one person! Can you imagine that? Amazing! No one had even called. You'd think that somebody like her would have family and friends. A homeless person would have been different. They're admitted all the time, and nobody cares whether they live or die. That's just how things go. Life's unfair. But not for somebody of such obvious refinement. And yet there she was.

"I took her vitals and asked her how she was feeling. She didn't remember much about the preceding night. All she could recount was going to a dinner party, where, she admitted, she'd drunk too much before catching a cab home. Everything else was a blur. She couldn't even remember her home address, family members or friends, or anything, really."

"How strange," I replied.

"Yeah, really strange. But then things got even stranger. The woman had two forms of ID on her, a driver's license and a credit card. Both were in different names. She couldn't reconcile this; in fact, she claimed both were correct. And when we asked her for her address or a point of contact, she couldn't recall. It was as if she had amnesia. Stranger still, the address on her license didn't exist, and her credit card was expired."

"So what did you do," I asked.

"First, the attending got her home address from the paramedics."

"How did they know?"

"How did they know? They got it from the concierge outside her building. He gave them her name, too. Still, that wasn't a lot to go on, so we reached out to the police in case anyone had contacted the authorities in search of her. None had."

"So?" I asked. "What happened?"

"Nothing."

"Nothing?"

"Nothing! That's the point."

"Oh, okay."

"She was totally abandoned. All alone."

"Right," I replied hesitantly.

For several moments, Gita did not speak, as if to allow time for the gravity of her story to take hold. It did not. "Livie, you don't get it, do you?" she said with exasperation.

I shook my head. "I guess not. It sounds like a sad story. Maybe the woman had some sort of alcohol-induced trauma. Or perhaps she suffered mental illness. I don't know. It's weird that she had no family calling on her, but I'm sure that the authorities will get to the bottom of it soon. She'll be fine."

"That's not the point," Gita responded sharply, prompting the cabbie to look at us in the rearview mirror. "The woman *will* be fine. She's probably got some rich family that will swoop in and retrieve her, take her back to some spacious Park Avenue duplex, and get her back on her meds. I'm sure it's not the first time it's happened to her."

"Why are you being so defensive?" I asked, irritated by Gita's righteous tone.

"Because, Livie, do I have to always spell things out to you?"

"Yeah, I guess you do. I didn't go to an Ivy League college," I shot back. "Remember? Enlighten me. Tell me the point."

"The poooiiint," she said in a drawn out, exaggerated tone, clearly irritated with me, "is that this woman had it all—looks, education, money. She was everything and more that anyone would want to be. She could've had a prestigious job. She could've hosted fancy dinners. She could've mingled with business leaders and celebrities. She could have been a star! But here she was in the ICU, having been scooped up by the paramedics after blacking out on the street. All that potential for admiration, adulation, and adoration wasted. Just wasted. It's so tragic."

The missed opportunity for high-society approval seemed of little consequence to me, but I was not going to argue the point. "Yeah," I said, "but she's going to be fine. Sounds like she comes from money, so I'm sure she'll be far better off than a homeless person who turns up at Lennox."

"Oh, forget it, Livie. You're from a different planet. It's not even worth it."

We sat silently for a minute, gazing out at Central Park as we bisected it from East Sixty-Fifth Street. "Let's say that I was picked up wandering the streets in dazed confusion. When you couldn't reach me, what would you do?"

"I'd call the police."

"Of course, you would. Anyone would. But then what?"

"What do you mean?" I asked.

"Oh, Livie, you're useless," Gita said, this time with resignation. "You'll always be useless."

"Yeah, you're right," I responded with similar resignation. "I'm useless. But promise me if you die in an ICU, I'll get first dibs on your apartment."

Gita laughed.

"And that I can date that hot resident friend of yours—Angelique? I think that's her name. I'd appreciate an introduction ahead of time."

"What am I going to do about you?" She smiled and leaned over to give me a kiss on the cheek. As I turned to face her, hoping to steal a kiss on the lips, she smiled and gently pushed me back. "None of that for you. You were late, remember?"

We alighted near Lincoln Center outside an Italian restaurant so crowded its patrons practically dined cheek by jowl. Gita, who had read that the establishment was popular with stars from a nearby television studio, demanded we stay put.

After a half-hour wait in a cramped foyer, we were finally seated near the back of the restaurant in front of an oil painting of a landscape. In washed-out greens and browns, the scene featured rolling hills dotted with Cyprus trees and a cottage with a terracotta-tiled roof. A small plaque on its frame read, "Toscana" or Tuscany. Nervous waiters in pressed white shirts and green aprons darted around the place, delivering hors d'oeuvres in a controlled chaos that contrasted with the soothing classical piano music piped over the speakers.

"Livie, wasn't it worth the wait?" Gita exclaimed while scanning the menu. "I think I'm going to drink some wine tonight. I deserve it."

"Yeah, you do. But if you get really sloppy and end up at Lennox in a boozy daze, I might not try all that hard to track you down. I'm useless, you know."

Gita laughed and leaned over to give me another kiss, this time on the lips. "Yes, you are. But occasionally you do make me laugh, so you're worth keeping around—for now."

With a certain truce apparently reached, we were able to enjoy our dinner, a grand affair with sumptuous appetizers, heaping plates of pasta, and creamy tiramisu for dessert. During the meal, Gita recounted various stories about her past week of residency, or "boot camp" as she called it, which were occasionally uplifting but more often not.

The practice of medicine seemed far less noble than Gita's sermonizing would suggest. It was, in fact, unsparingly brutal and cruel work. The attending physicians were akin to drill instructors—hence the boot camp metaphor—who seemed to revel in belittling the grunts. Gita and her fellow residents were overworked, overstressed, and overwrought. Two had had nervous breakdowns over that past year. One had quit her residency altogether. Five years earlier, a resident in the same program had killed herself using stolen painkillers.

After recounting a long night that had culminated in a vicious dressing-down by the attending, Gita, now revived, suggested we take a walk despite the overcast skies. We headed for Lincoln Center before crossing Eighth Avenue toward Columbus Circle.

The streets glistened with the city's lights reflecting off the wet pavement. The thoroughfares, whose poor state of repair was conspicuous by day, were rendered wondrous on a rainy night. Gotham was like an ancient artifact best viewed in reduced light to obscure its many imperfections.

As we approached Columbus Circle hand in hand, we began hearing a low rhythmic bass. It grew louder and more menacing as we got closer to the circle and saw a crowd had gathered. When we arrived, the palpitating's provenance became clear: hundreds of Comitans were chanting, led by a smaller group standing on an impromptu stage erected in the middle of the circle. "Hey, hey, ho, ho, collectivists have to go." They jumped in rhythm. Several kept the beat by vigorously banging massive drums, while another sometimes let it rip by blowing an air horn.

Many held "I am John Galt" placards, while others waved the group's yellow eagle-bearing standard. A few waved Confederate flags. A line of officers in riot gear stood at attention around the circle's circumference.

Across the street, near the entrance to Central Park, a small counterdemonstration, comprising several dozen protestors, stood listlessly with their own handmade signs. "The Right Is Wrong," one read. Another, oddly, "Let's figure this shit out together." Occasionally, they traded insults with the Comitans, but mostly they stood in silence, observing their antagonists from a comfortable distance. A few passersby managed to get a rise out of them by shouting their support or offering high fives, prompting boisterous cheers or fist pumps. However, the enthusiasm proved fleeting, and the group, apparently demoralized by being far outnumbered, soon quieted—meek resistance.

"Livie, they're so obnoxious. They're making so much noise. What are they complaining about anyway?"

"They're Comitans," I answered.

"Who?"

"Comitans."

"Who are they?"

I wondered what to say.

Gita's principled intellectual illiteracy had been put to the test when the market first tanked and the country was enveloped by dread. In an uncharacteristically inquisitive moment, she had asked about the origins of the crisis as we passed a line of people outside a soup kitchen. I wondered whether the scales had fallen from her eyes—unpleasant realities disrupting her sheltered life. Circumstances had changed—and possibly changed her. Perhaps now she would begin to take an interest in the world beyond medicine, or so I hoped.

From Gita's exclusive upbringing capped by an Ivy League diploma, she exemplified a life full of possibility—and she would deliver. Yet for all her accomplishments, she had never emerged from her gilded cocoon, with one exception: a rotation in an inner-city hospital during medical school. The experience had dissuaded her from working with the underprivileged. "It's just not for me," she explained. "That patient population isn't for me. I need to feel like my efforts are appreciated by people who are as committed to helping themselves as I am to helping them."

Her unexpected curiosity on this occasion fed my ego. Ordinarily, Gita was indifferent to my areas of expertise and rarely sought to tap them. Consequently, I had taken delight in fashioning a thorough response that day outside the soup kitchen, referencing the economic policies precipitating the crash before starting in on the crisis itself. As I was holding forth, Gita suddenly squeaked with delight at a passing shih tzu.

"Oh, the little guy is so cute," she chirped, bending down to pet the small dog. When its owner moved on, I resumed my explanation, but the moment had passed. Having poked her head above the parapet to take a look around at the great expanse before her, she had now crouched down again, content in the battlement.

Gita had interjected as I attempted to continue my explanation. "Oh, Livie, please," she whined. "Politics is so…so *political*. It's so fake. And meaningless. I really don't understand why anyone would spend any time on it. It's good that you left Washington."

And that was that. Never had she inquired again about current events or anything with a hint of the cerebral unrelated to medicine. Until now.

"They're fanatics," I began explaining, tentatively at first. "The Comitans formed at a Patriot Posse convention around the time of the financial meltdown. They think that the root of our problems is that we have too many immigrants and too much government. They've always existed in some form, but—"

"Livie," Gita interjected. "Patriot Posse? Comitans? I didn't want a lecture. You know how much I hate all that stuff. How many times to do I have to tell you? Why don't people just carry on with their own lives without getting caught up in such theatrics?"

"Because politics *matters*," I answered sternly. "Practically everything is political. Even medicine."

Gita did not respond.

"Really, Gita, think about it. Who delivers healthcare? Private insurers or the government. How much money should be put into medical R&D? How do we cover the elderly and poor? What—"

"You're lecturing again. I want to go home."

I made another attempt to continue, but she was firm, so we retreated back to the way we came in silence, leaving the angry Comitans behind in Columbus Circle. She then requested a car on her ride-hailing app. As her vehicle approached, I asked, "Can

I come over?" We may not have had much of an intellectual connection, but that did not preclude a physical one. That was a virtue of being placeholders.

"I don't think so. I'm tired. Plus, I have to work early."

I was not surprised. A litany of transgressions—my lack of punctuality, my nonchalance about her patient, my political pontificating, and so on—had earned this punishment. I was being taught a lesson. I would be celibate as long as I continued to "lecture."

I embraced Gita and gave her a kiss on the cheek before she ducked into the vehicle. "Bye, Livie," she uttered without emotion.

I closed the door and watched the cab disappear to the accompaniment of Comitan chanting. The rain, dark and sporadic, resumed.

CHAPTER 4

DOWN THE RABBIT HOLE

Friday, 6:20 p.m. Ten minutes to freedom. All the other 10,079 minutes of the workweek began to melt away in glorious irrelevance. Let the weekend countdown begin. I basked in the expectation of uninterrupted sleep, social engagements, and freedom from in-box tyranny and toxic office politics.

To live to escape that which consumes a majority of one's waking hours is one of life's cruel peculiarities. Our ancestors supposedly labored between twenty and forty hours a week hunting and foraging for food. Yet, despite miraculous technological, economic, and cultural advances, we actually work longer hours today—and often in unfulfilling and unnecessary jobs, as Alex had pointed out.

Of course, everything is relative. Office work beats the salt mines. It is also far less miserable than no job at all—an emasculated, anxious state with no remedy but gainful employment. But this doesn't diminish the misery of the average office job. Constipation may be a mere inconvenience compared with the Bubonic plague, but try telling yourself that the next time you're experiencing wrenching indigestion after ordering chicken tikka masala from the corner food truck. At that point, you may actually wish you had the medieval scourge, which at least offered permanent relief.

As was my 6:20 p.m. ritual, I began organizing the papers on my desk, turning off the computer, and gathering my belongings. The weekend was at hand.

"Liv." The British-accent was unmistakable as I gathered my belongings. "I'm glad I caught you. Do you have a minute?" Mortimer asked.

"Of course." I hoped he could not hear my annoyance at being corralled as I was about to make my escape or my alarm as to why he had done so. Was it the quality of my work? Had I said something offensive? Was I going to be fired?

We walked back to his office and closed the door.

"I hope I'm not keeping you from an engagement," Mortimer said cheerily.

"No, not at all."

"Good. I wanted to commend you on the work you did for the MalayNG account. I didn't get around to pointing out how satisfied I was. Your backgrounder and the follow-on case study helped us get the contract renewed. That's no small matter during times like these."

"Thank you," I answered. "It was a team effort. Michael played a big role, the biggest role, to be honest. His analysis of price variation was key."

This was true. Michael's contribution, as always, was indispensible. But I felt bad for his being bumped off the trip out West to meet with MalayNG's executive team and for not being more sympathetic when he had dropped by my cubicle to vent about it weeks earlier. Singing his praises was the least I could do.

"Yes, it was. Michael is a big asset. But your ability to collate large data sets and summarize varied and disparate information—coupled with a knack for presenting them in an accessible format—well, that made all the difference. We wouldn't have won the account without it. And I particularly appreciate how you were able to pull it all together under a tight deadline. This will be noted in your upcoming performance appraisal, Liv."

"Thank you," I responded. The compliment felt good, especially in light of my concern as to why Mortimer wanted to speak to me. Yet the sense of pride proved fleeting. Apathy was my enduring reaction, which begged the question: Does doing a good job matter if one doesn't care about the job in the first place? I wasn't sure.

"Now, I did want to briefly raise another matter, the Eco-Excellence campaign. It's come to my attention that you've got the office's second-lowest rating."

The "rating" in question purportedly reflected each employee's carbon footprint on a comparative basis. I was near the bottom. How was the footprint gauged? Marcy used a measure circulating on the web that took into account energy use from transportation, food production, and other activities, along with other measures assessing consumption patterns. It was hopelessly crude.

Yet Mortimer and other senior managers had adopted it, even adding the inducement of a bonus to the employee with the highest rating. I dismissed the do-good exercise as harmless at best. It was just about PR. I could not be bothered.

"You are aware of your rating?" Mortimer asked, a hint of disapproval in his voice.

"Yes, of course."

"I want to emphasize that the campaign is voluntary. You're

encouraged, not required, to participate. Yet I, along with Oliver, Allen, and the rest of the executive team, all enthusiastically support the initiative and encourage everyone to participate. Did you know that it's actually getting press attention? *Finance Today* is going to do a feature on it. They've already interviewed Marcy, and they're sending a cameraman over next week to get some photos to accompany their piece.

"We're very proud of what Marcy has done and think it's a way of promoting environmental stewardship and, well, promoting ourselves too. This is going to help raise our profile. You're free to do as you please, Liv, but I hope that we can get 100 percent engagement from you on this."

"I understand," I replied. "I haven't paid attention to the campaign because I've been rather busy with MalayNG and, more recently, the SYNAC account. And to be honest, I am not all that confident that the rating actually reflects our carbon footprint, which seems rather hard to quantify."

"Quite right, Liv. The rating is very imprecise. But let's not make the perfect the enemy of the good. What we're trying to do, what Marcy has been trying to do, is promote awareness. Thinking about ways in which we can contribute to a greener environment is half the battle. It's sort of a reminder, an omniscient eye."

"Omniscient eye?"

"Let me put it like this: behavior is contingent on the perception of being monitored. People are far more likely to come to the aid of another person if others witness it. Recognition is key. We all act more selflessly when we expect a reward for doing so. We're all suckers for good publicity."

Perhaps sensing my confusion, Mortimer elaborated.

"Hospitals, for example, have found that handwashing by doctors and nurses rises when official notices are placed above sink stations. The impression of being watched increases compliance. Hence the 'omniscient eye.'"

"See what I'm getting at, Liv? It's not the rating's accuracy that's important, it's that it's made public. That's what most likely will induce behavioral change. Make sense?"

I thought better of pointing out that public shaming had no impact on my participation in Marcy's fruitless exercise. I was against it on principle. It was dumb.

"I would be remiss if I didn't mention that Marcy has done a lot of work to put together this campaign, so it's only fair that we give it an honest go. You agree, don't you?"

"Yes," I said with the all the conviction I could muster.

"Great then, I look forward to your full participation beginning Monday. I'm delighted that we had this chance to chat. I trust I haven't taken too much of your time."

"No, not at all."

"That's good. Do have a pleasant weekend then." Mortimer stood up and shook my hand. "Keep up the solid work."

I thanked Mortimer and exited the building quickly. When I turned the corner and crossed Bryant Park, I noticed a text from Alex postponing our planned get-together. "Money never sleeps, and neither do thieves," the text read. "Gotta rip off Brazilian retirees. Last-minute tasking. Sorry. Let's reschedule."

No matter, I thought. I called Gita on the off chance she would be free, but she immediately complained about being overwhelmed at work. After scolding me for not reaching out earlier to check in on her, she muttered a few expletives about her attending before signing off. "I'm too busy to talk. Sorry, Livie."

I ducked into the subway as it began to drizzle.

Minutes after I arrived home, the skies opened up. Perhaps I should spend the weekend building that ark. It might be prudent after all, given the biblical levels of rainfall that the city had endured lately. Even the Comitans had picked up on the theme; one of their leaders claimed that God was signaling His displeasure.

As I opened my apartment door, a blast of heat slammed into me as if I had teleported to Hawaii. Though new and well apportioned, the building was riddled by faulty heating. Adjusting the thermostat was futile. I opened a window immediately. A breeze caught my photo of Franz Kafka and caused it to shimmy slightly on my otherwise barren wall. In black and white, the writer appeared to be in his twenties. Wearing a dress shirt, ascot, overcoat, and bowler hat, he stared directly at the camera with a slight smile, a dog by his side. He was vigorous and handsome, ready to face the world. In the end, though, the world conquered Kafka. Physical and psychological maladies cut him down at forty, his genius as yet unrecognized. It was foreboding.

The portrait moved me. I once had literary ambitions of my own. I began writing in my teens. At first, it was simply a pleasant hobby, but in due course it became much more, a necessary release valve for the frustrations and absurdities in my life—silly social conventions, vapid love interests, pointless jobs. I suspected writing had served a similar purpose for Kafka, who suffered an unsupportive mother, tyrannical father, and a tedious job as an insurance adjuster.

For years, I maintained a steady output of articles for a friend's website. I graduated to short stories, one of which was published in the *Cornhusker Review*, a Nebraska-based literary magazine. Only later did I learn that its circulation barely cracked triple digits. It did not matter. I was now a published author. Every journey begins with a small step, so it goes. As my literary confidence grew, so did my ambitions. Eventually, I began a novel, a coming-of-age story inspired by my own faltering efforts to find meaning in a cynical world. As the cliché went, I wrote what I knew.

Yet unlike Kafka, whose everyday burdens fed his literary drive, mine overwhelmed it. My output plummeted along with my morale, undermined by personal and professional setbacks. On those rare occasions when I wrote these days, little of merit resulted. My manuscript sat unfinished, yet another reminder of my unrealized potential.

The rest of the one-bedroom apartment was largely empty. The small living area had a circular wood table surrounded by two matching chairs, along with a small, pillowless couch facing Kafka's portrait. The room was otherwise bare. The kitchen was nested in a corner and featured a small and rarely used range and refrigerator. My bedroom was effectively a closet with a bed and the bathroom a Porta Potty with a shower stall. The entire place was testament to my aesthetic indifference.

Gita, seeing my apartment for the first time, had asked whether it was a short-term rental. She did not approve. That I lived on the West and not the East Side was my first demerit. That I lived in a nice, though not exclusive, building was my second demerit. And the lifeless state of my décor in what appeared to be an unoccupied shell was my third.

Two weeks into our relationship, she'd left a note on my dining room table: "What you need." It itemized the need for furniture, a car, a Hamptons timeshare, and a classy suit. Below, it stated, "You are no longer a college student. Raise your game. It's time to live."

I *was* living, even if apathetically. I didn't care about my living environment because I didn't plan to plant roots in New York. Or anywhere. I existed day to day. What suited me in the moment, suited me. My morale did not permit longer time horizons.

I settled in for an evening at home and ordered Chinese take-out. While I was eating, my phone rang. It was my father.

"Liv, I'm glad I reached you. I tried last night, but you weren't around. You know how frustrated I get when I can't get hold of you. You really have to make yourself available."

"Sorry, Dad. I've been busy."

"That's no excuse. Anyway, I didn't call to yell at you. That's your mother's job." He laughed briefly at his own joke. "Tell me how work is going. And how's Gina?"

"Gita," I corrected.

"Yes, of course. How's she doing? Is she still working hard? I don't know how doctors do it, especially surgeons. Their hours are brutal."

"Dad, Gita's not a surgeon."

"Oh? I thought she was."

"She did a surgical rotation a while back, but she's a second-year internal med resident."

"Right. Anyway, send her my regards. I hope to meet her someday. So, Liv, I'm calling to tell you that your mother and I are moving."

"Really? Where to this time?" I responded cynically.

My father paused. "You know your mother and I are very proud of you, Liv, and what you've accomplished professionally. But your work is very different from mine. Educators like me don't stay in one place. We're not like nine-to-fivers. It's just the way things are.

"We've decided to leave Beloit," he added, referencing the small college town in southern Wisconsin and eponymous college. "The school's philosophy just doesn't align with ours anymore. Too much emphasis on 'practical' courses like accounting and finance. I miss the experimental learning. That's what originally drew your mother and me to the school. It's clear to us now that the college has abandoned its liberal arts tradition, like so many others. It's just a glorified technical school now, a giant stamping machine that produces robots ready to analyze corporate spreadsheets and produce PowerPoint presentations. What happened to nurturing creativity? What happened to learning for learning's sake?"

"I don't know, Dad. College can be about exploring intellectual horizons. It was for me. And it certainly was for you and Mom. But how many college students are interested in learning? Not many. Most just want to drink and party, so why not help prepare them for the job market when the music stops?"

"Prepare them for the job market?" my father repeated my words in disbelief. "We've lost our way, Liv." He then went on a ten-minute riff about education being the bedrock of democracy and how the educational crisis meant democracy was in crisis. I'd heard this rant many times before.

"You're an idealist, Dad. What about the tutoring for high school students? I thought you had gotten really into that."

"I'm still doing it. It's very rewarding. And I'll continue doing it, just not here in Wisconsin. We've made up our minds."

"So where are you going?

"Whittier."

"Whittier?" I repeated. "Where's that?"

"Southern California, about equidistant between LA and

Anaheim. It's home to Whittier College, a small liberal arts school founded by Quakers. Its philosophy seems more in keeping with my own. Of course, Nixon went there, but even diamonds have imperfections."

"Oh, I see. Has the school hired you yet?"

"Yes, of course. Do you think we'd just pick up stakes without a plan? They've even offered your mother a part-time job in the admissions office, though she's still deciding whether she wants to make that commitment, seeing how it'll take her away from her poetry—"

My mother interjected. "Liv, is that you?"

"Hi Mom. How are you?"

"Good. I gather your father has told you the news already. It may sound sudden, but I assure you it's not. Your father and I have been thinking about this for some time now. We need to regenerate. An unchallenged life is no life at all.

It's not as if we dislike it here. Your father has enjoyed his introductory classes, and his volunteer work at a local high school has been a success. You know how much he relishes working with adolescents. I don't know why he doesn't dedicate himself to teaching kids full time. He'd be so much happier."

"How's your poetry these days, Mom?"

"I've found a wonderful poetry group. It has been so formative, even though we meet only every other week. My technique has improved immeasurably. In fact, I'm thinking about trying to publish the poems I've written. Well, that's the plan anyway. My painting has gotten so much better, too. I'm taking lessons. Elaine, my teacher, is a brilliant artist—shows in New York and Boston. She says that I'm one of the quickest studies she's ever seen. She's encouraging me to explore my creative potential, so

I've been doing a lot of pointillist work recently. Elaine says I've got a little Impressionist in me. Can you imagine that?"

"That's great, Mom," I observed, barely breaking her momentum. The risk of such was negligible; like a large oceangoing vessel, my mother, once steaming forward at full speed, was not easily halted. She went on for a while about painting and then transitioned seamlessly into a long-winded riff about Southern California's great weather and other creative outlets.

"That's great, Mom," I repeated, my praise functioning as a verbal green light endorsing her monologue's onward march. Such "conversations" recalled one comic's standup routine about his being unable to return home for Thanksgiving. He therefore suggests to his grandmother that she record him then and there and replay the footage on her television during the holiday meal as an alternative. "On the count of three," he explains, "start recording."

Moments later, with an earnest gaze, he says, "Oh, I see. Yes. Yes. Okay." He then pauses for several moments before adding, "You don't say. He didn't! I can't believe it. Oh, no. No! Really?"

I was like the comic. When it came to dialoguing with my mother, I was a mere avatar.

My mother continued uninterrupted for ten more minutes while I tuned out. Then suddenly she asked how I was.

"I'm fine, Mom. Work is going okay, and I—"

"Oh, that reminds me," she interrupted. "I'm sorry, but I must tell you before I forget: we're selling the boat."

Another ten-minute riff followed, until once again she asked, "What about Rita? She's a surgeon, no?"

"She's fine," I answered, not bothering to correct her. Talking to my mother—or rather, listening to my mother—was a draining experience. The fatigue was all the more remarkable considering how little I actually participated in the event.

"Gita's working hard. All residents work hard. It's a rite of passage. I don't see her much. Otherwise everything's fine. Nothing to report."

"Well, that's a shame. But I guess no news is good news."

I concurred. We wished each other well and promised to speak soon. Chore complete.

The news of my parents' latest move was no surprise. On the contrary, it was expected. That they had stayed put in Wisconsin for five years was remarkable. When I was born, my parents were living in Terre Haute, Indiana, where my father was an associate professor of English literature at one of the state universities. Before I turned two, we had moved to Boise, Idaho. The places we called home after that were a jumble of college towns, each serene and rustic. There was Northfield, Minnesota; Decorah, Indiana; Gambier, Ohio; Sewanee, Tennessee; Waterville, Maine; Johnson, Vermont; Easton, Pennsylvania; Lexington, Virginia; and Poughkeepsie, New York, among others. The passage of time had rendered these destinations indistinguishable. Family photos from my childhood were marked with the date and, critically, location.

Invariably, after a few years in one location, my father would breach a personal threshold, and proclaim the need to "replace the spent creative rods." A move would follow shortly thereafter, but the pattern continued: a town, a new position, and enthusiastic and engaged students. But the honeymoon never lasted. My father's principled refusal to play office politics always sealed his fate. Like an organ introduced into a foreign body, he faced rejection from contemptuous colleagues threatened by this subversive interloper. It did not take long for the antibodies to strike—three years, max.

The nomadic lifestyle suited my mother just fine. "Moving every few years allows me to prosper," she once volunteered, referencing her ever-evolving flirtation with artistic undertakings—ceramics, etching, needlepoint, tapestries, poetry, and so on—that conveniently substituted for any real career of her own. "I wouldn't have become the person I am."

Even my ridiculous name reflected my parents' free-spiritedness. The two had met in college and, after graduation, served together in the Peace Corps in Africa. The experience had instilled an enduring love for the continent as well as reverence for the nineteenth-century Scottish missionary, David Livingstone.

The London Missionary Society had posted Livingstone to southern Africa in the early 1840s. From his base on the rim of the Kalahari Desert, he'd made daring journeys into the continent's uncharted interior. Over the course of three decades, he had crossed central Africa—a first for a Westerner—found Victoria Falls, searched for the source of the Nile, and "saved" natives' souls.

A product of his times—though frightfully ethnocentric by ours—Livingstone embodied an audacity and pluck that my parents admired. That was their logic for my first name, which I don't like...no, I despise it. It is so patrician. Put an aristocratic title before it, followed by a stuffy-sounding place in England, and you might form the name of a character from a Jane Austen novel. It's enough to get the blood boiling. While adopting the diminutive "Liv" helps, I still feel cursed.

I guess everyone has their cross to bear. Mine is my name. And my parents—they're exhausting. I always feel like napping after we speak. There probably is some psychological reason for this, though I cannot figure it out. Whatever the explanation, I try to avoid such conversations early in the evening, as I struggle to keep my eyes open afterward. Tonight was no different. But it was too early to go to bed, so I turned on the Knicks game to revive myself and reheated the remainder of my Chinese take-out. It wasn't a thrilling game, so at halftime I opened a highly acclaimed novel I'd purchased at the airport during a business trip a few months earlier. There was a ton of buzz around the book and it was going to be made into a film. Even Gita, never one for casual reading, had recommended it, having devoured it during a beach vacation.

I hadn't made much progress on it. This was partly because I had the habit of picking it up after I spoke to my parents and thus promptly would fall asleep. But the novel was lousy, too. It was predictable and snobby. That I had managed to get through the first fifty pages was an accomplishment. With great effort, I tried to plow through a couple of chapters before reaching my wit's end when the protagonist, a Harvard-educated twenty-something, quits his job teaching on an Indian reservation to enter medical school. I could see why it spoke to Gita. I put the book down and turned off the Knicks game. It was getting late and I was exhausted. Yet, I felt strangely restless. I leaned back and closed my eyes. I had not tried meditating in months.

Years earlier, during a rough patch, I had sought out therapy. I hadn't gotten much out of it, so I stopped going after several ses-sions. However, my short stint in analysis did prompt me to take up meditation, something the therapist had suggested, claiming it would help reduce stress and could potentially yield unexpected self-awareness. It seemed like an odd recommendation, but I tried it anyway.

I was instructed to concentrate on the mental image of myself stretched out on a deserted beach, waves gently lapping the shore nearby. Each time, a strange transformation took place. A crying infant appeared in my stead, transforming the serene scene into one of alarm and horror. The wailing, isolated baby appeared on the sand repeatedly. I kept trying, but meditation was not an avenue to serenity for me. But I felt strangely out of sorts tonight, so I began inhaling through my nose and exhaling via pursed lips. I slowed my respiration, and tried to clear my mental clutter. I imagined myself sitting on an empty beach, listening to the sound of the waves lapping on the shore. Peaceful.

The sea at dusk was nearly motionless, an ebony slate stretching to the horizon, with only modest wave action near the shore. A seagull floated silently overhead on an upward draft. Transported to this tranquil seaside setting, I inhaled the salty air while listening intently to the gently breaking waves. All was quiet. A feeling of buoyancy overcame me, as if I were being released from gravity's grip and might slowly ascend upward.

In an instant, a baby's cry again interrupted my interlude. At first it was barely audible, but then grew into a grating timbre, overwhelming my powers of concentration. I could not shut the damn thing out. As my focus was diverted by the child's wailing, I realized, as I had many times before during such moments of interrupted meditation, that I was the disconsolate infant. I was the naked baby, legs kicking and tears cascading—pleading for what, I did not know.

"Screw it," I mumbled. I rose to my feet, turned out the lights, and retreated to my bedroom where I fell asleep in minutes. My subconscious, though, flickered and gyrated on. I was haunted by a dream during which I was walking down a railroad track on a high desert plain. It was oppressively hot. My shirt was soaked with perspiration. Buzzards flew overhead. The sound of a train's whistle blared, at first in the distance. As it grew closer, its jarring ring grew intolerable, just like the baby's wailing. I began to walk faster, then trot, and finally sprint as the black locomotive approached. I could not outrun it, I knew, but I could not leave the track.

I was trapped.

As the massive engine bore down on me, the cobra-like hissing of its steam engine grew intense. Still running, I repeatedly turned my head to check its horrible progress. Then, suddenly, the track before me ended at a cliff. I could turn and be overrun by the screaming train or jump off the precipice. The choice was mine.

I woke up drenched in sweat.

CHAPTER 5

STRICKLAND

had made it through another week. Precisely seventy-one days had passed since that crappy meeting when Marcy launched the Eco-Excellence campaign. I had counted. Did it matter? Probably not. One day segued to another without distinction. It was eerie. Was a lifetime simply the sum total of banal recollections accrued from one ordinary day to the next?

Today, I hoped, was different—it was Friday. I was counting down the minutes…6:18, 6:19, 6:20! Mercifully, the week's winddown point had arrived. Per my Friday ritual, I began shutting down my computer and organizing my belongings, grinning all the while.

"Why are you so happy?" Brilliant Brad asked as he moseyed by my cubicle, his tie askew and white shirt untucked. Slovenliness was an unpardonable sin in the corporate world, but Brilliant Brad's considerable smarts provided absolution. "I wish I was as giddy as you to get outta here, but I have to come in over the weekend to finish up the Durant projections. No rest for the weary."

"Well, to whom much talent is given, much is expected."

"That's one way of putting it." Brilliant Brad wiped his nose with his sleeve. "It's actually to whom much bullshit is given, much bullshit is expected. And trust me, I will deliver." He shook a forefinger at me with a cocky smile.

"You always do."

"Yeah, I should get an Oscar for Best Actor in a Comedy." He shrugged and skulked off to his cubicle.

Hustling toward the elevator bank, I scanned left and right like a squirrel on the lookout for predators. If Mortimer was on the prowl, I did not want to be cornered about my lagging Eco-Excellence ratings. I simply could not generate the requisite enthusiasm for Marcy's ridiculous project, even though climbing the corporate ranks required playing the game. I knew the shtick—you have to brownnose, schmooze. Success is contingent on your boss identifying in you the same brazen pandering that propelled his or her ascent. It's a sort of species recognition. Only then are you deemed management material. I did not care.

The elevator seemed to take an eternity to appear, prompting me to mutter a curse, but I was spared an encounter with Mortimer. After descending to the lobby from Marshall Cooper's offices on the thirty-sixth floor, I was propelled into a stampede of exultant nine-to-fivers fleeing as if the popular all-you-can-eat Chinese buffet across the street were running a free promotion. Careful not to be crushed, I hurried outside and made my way to the subway. I was home in twenty-eight minutes flat, a near record.

It was Friday and, for once, not raining.

Perfection.

"We're on," read Alex's text, which arrived as I undid my noose-like tie. "My place. Topic: women."

It had been months since Alex had called off his last all-guy get-together. These were a tradition along the lines of a bris insofar as both featured drinking, reverie, and ritual laceration—in Alex's case, of the verbal variety. Their thin intellectual pretentions inevitably succumbed to alcohol-induced debauchery. In one memorable case, a discussion about a preassigned book was forgotten entirely when it turned out that the evening dovetailed with the NBA playoffs. This was typical. They were more saloon than salon.

After showering and changing into jeans and T-shirt, I made my way to Tribeca, where Alex lived in a former factory. His building's cast-iron facade had metal overhangs painted orange, under which trucks had once loaded all manner of goods—carpets, garments, meat, produce—for transport around the city and to the dockyards for shipment around the world.

The elegantly constructed edifice had gone up when pride of place existed. It was an age of ascendance, and investments were made with the assurance of better times ahead. America's century had loomed.

The aging gems, however, long since hollowed out by deindustrialization, had fallen into disrepair. During the seedy seventies, around the time the city had gone bankrupt, the whole area was an urban wasteland, even though it was situated just blocks from Wall Street's global commerce. Entire city blocks in the area had been laid to waste, a sort of post-apocalyptic tableau littered with the remnants of once-proud buildings. The nearby parks had become havens for the homeless. Ghettos had blossomed. Slowly, though, the area had been revitalized. First, artists in search of cheap rents had moved in, followed by young hipsters and eventually, as gentrification picked up steam, moneyed professionals.

Alex opened his door wearing a preppy tie over a Hawaiian shirt, cargo pants, and flip-flops. Around his forehead was a translucent, red-shaded visor. He looked like a fraternity brother at homecoming.

"I can see you're ready for a night of serious intellectual exploration, Alex."

"Liv!" he yelled, enveloping me in a bear hug with those long arms. "So glad you made it! You know the ground rules: what's said here can and will be used against you in a court of law. Come in and grab some food. And a beer—or twelve."

I pushed my way into Alex's glorious loft. Remnants of early evening sunlight poured through the floor-to-ceiling windows, illuminating the main room and its large table, matching seats, and vacant bookshelf abutting an exposed brick wall. There hung a single, framed picture of a surfer kneeling beneath a gigantic wave's turquoise arc.

Roughly fifteen guests were mingling in groups of two or three. A few pizza boxes were stacked on the table, opposite an array of bottles of wines and spirits and a large plastic bin filled with cans of beer on ice. Classic rock was emanating from overhead speakers.

I helped myself to a beer and scanned the assembled for familiar faces. I headed toward the one person I recognized, Strickland, a childhood friend of Alex's whom I had met at a previous get-together where he'd nearly sparked a riot by casually suggesting that America was run by and for the rich. Royce, a hawk-nosed mutual fund manager with a hair-trigger temper, had gone ballistic. With a flushed face, he'd launched into a vicious diatribe, accusing Strickland of inexcusable naiveté, if not worse.

"Of course our government is flawed," he'd hollered. "But to suggest that it does not reflect the people's will is laughable. Artists are permitted to live in fantasy worlds of their own making. The rest of us, not so much."

Strickland had responded calmly, offering up a thoughtful counterargument about the influence of money on all aspects of society. On a host of issues, he'd said, naming several, those with legislative power catered to the desires of wealthy Americans and interests rather than those of the average voter. "That's called oligarchy," Strickland had observed coolly.

Strickland's calm had only fed his antagonist's anger, and with each rhetorical salvo, Royce grew more furious. But for the timely arrival of a dozen more guests, who'd quickly shifted the party's focus away from politics, the affair might have ended up in fisticuffs.

Strickland, whom everyone addressed by his surname for some unknown reason, did not look the part of a rabble-rouser. Of average stature, he had a sallow face with unexceptional features: brown, slightly plaintive eyes that sat above a delicate, sloping nose, thin lips, and a receding chin. His closely clipped blond hair was styled to television-anchor perfection. His average physical appearance effectively camouflaged his unorthodox ideas—until he opened his mouth.

He and Alex had moved to New York together after college, and both had gone into finance at rival banks. Strickland's professional ascent was as dramatic as Alex's, as he shared his friend's exceptional intelligence. Within three years, he was promoted twice. Strickland's annual bonus his fourth year was so lucrative he bought his parents a vacation house. Fourteen months later, Strickland was made the bank's youngest division chief ever. Just weeks after that, he quit abruptly.

Alex was stunned, as was everyone who knew Strickland. His boss, after offering him a large financial inducement to stay on, prevailed on the CEO to make a personal intervention. Nothing changed Strickland's mind. He was determined to go.

Strickland never provided a full explanation for his odd decision, aside from his desire to "pursue other life goals." But within weeks of leaving, he had moved out of his exclusive Midtown penthouse into a pokey studio in Brooklyn, where he began painting.

Even those who knew Strickland well, and were aware of his long-standing interest in the visual arts, were convinced he had taken leave of his senses. Who in his right mind, after all, quits a highly compensated Wall Street job…to paint? It was insane.

Most of his friends anticipated he would be sending out resumes by year's end, once he had gotten the art bug out of his system. Several months later, Alex, convinced his friend had made a catastrophic mistake, offered to find him a gig at his bank, but Strickland declined. His mind was made up. "It's not that I want to paint. I need to paint. There's no choice."

What seemed like an ill-conceived decision, widely presumed to have been prompted by finance's grueling pace, or perhaps some psychological illness, gained credibility at Strickland's first show two years later. The venue was a small café near his Brooklyn apartment, far from SoHo's glamorous galleries. It hardly mattered. Strickland's talent was undeniable, even to those with little art appreciation. His paintings featured dazzling images and themes of impending violence and doom. In one, a sneering businessman with slicked-back hair, prominent brow, and serrated teeth concealed a knife behind his back while peering down menacingly at a cowering subordinate hunched over a computer.

In another, a giant thresher with blades dripping with blood bore down on crop-picking Hispanic laborers, who were unaware of the danger.

The largest depicted a dystopian landscape: a crop of glass skyscrapers interspersed with industrial smokestacks growing weed-like toward a dark sky. Out of the bellowing chimneys spewed a mixture of ash and burning currency that fell onto a green landscape, turning it mud brown. Strickland's sentiments regarding his former life were clearly on display for all to see.

The arresting work's radical political commentary and its almost cartoonish imagery, violent themes, and pastel colors overwhelmed the audience's senses. It bore similarity to the iconic Mexican muralists, such as Diego Rivera and José Clemente Orozco, whose provocative paintings also featured nationalistic, political, and social themes. Like their powerful work, his had all the subtlety of a sledgehammer meeting pavement.

Despite the disturbing subject matter, each canvas drew you in. It tapped into the same morbid curiosity that prompts rubbernecking at the scene of an accident. The work was mesmerizing. Attention had to be paid.

Even with all his talent and after several years, starting a conversation with Strickland was still awkward. He had made a transition so foreign to all of us that we did not know how to start a regular conversation with him. I felt strangely inadequate. I feared he would see me as a corporate shill with little to offer. Yet, he was the only person beside Alex I recognized, so I decided to dive in.

"How's your painting coming?" I inquired, reminding him we had met at one of Alex's earlier parties.

"Okay. Well, not really. It's very hard. Nothing I've done is harder. Not even close."

He described suffering a sort of writer's block, an artistic paralysis that led him to spend hours in front of a canvas unable to execute a single brushstroke. "By day's end on such occasions, I'm dead tired, even though I've done nothing. It's like feeling as though you've run a marathon without having left your bed. I recall some writer saying something about how he hated writing but loved having written. That's how I feel about painting. Doing it is misery; having done it is bliss. And yet I can't stop."

I told him about my fleeting dream to be a writer, adding that, unlike him, I had never had the courage to try and realize my dream. I was a hobbyist, nothing more. He was the genuine article. "I guess that's what separates artists from the rest of us. Artists dare to plunge into the unknown."

Strickland laughed. "That's very romantic. You don't hear about the thousands of artists who give flight to their creative ambitions only to return to more conventional lives once they see what it's like. More traditional professions have their merits. Trust me, I know."

"Well, what do you know, if it isn't Karl Marx," a voice ripe with condescension rang out. "Shouldn't you be plotting the workers' revolution?" Royce approached and slapped Strickland on the shoulder in a gesture of feigned camaraderie. "I'm just kidding," he added unconvincingly. "Good to see you again."

Strickland smiled faintly. "Good to see you, too."

"Liv," Alex called out, waving his massive mitts at me from across the room. "Come here for a moment. I want you to meet someone. This is Marco," he said as I neared. "He works with me.

Well, down the hall, to be exact. You guys must've overlapped at the Treasury Department."

Marco was tall and skinny with two probing eyes set above a pronounced mouth that gave him a sort of avian appearance. He had in fact worked at the government department at the same time as me, though in a different office. He knew a few of my former colleagues as well as some other acquaintances. We traded our impressions of government work for some time before a heated discussion on the opposite side of the room attracted our attention. Alex's apartment was now full of guests, but most had congregated around where the stormy atmospherics were emanating. Marco and I, our curiosity piqued, headed over.

"Are you serious?" Royce asked with disbelief. "You're single and don't date? Are you a monk?"

Strickland, who had not moved from the chair he'd occupied earlier, was unruffled by the sharp questioning. "Well, sort of," he replied with typical stoicism. "I occasionally leave the monastery, my studio. I just don't waste a lot of time when I do."

The two were going at it again. This is why we were here. Alex's gatherings could be like prizefights. Mostly, the topic of a given debate—some arcane matter—was incidental. What mattered was the cut and thrust, the spectacle. It was street fighting for nerds. But occasionally it was more than that. Sometimes ideas actually mattered. This appeared to be one of those times. It was the main event. Alex might've announced, "Get ready to rumble!"

"What do you mean, 'waste time?'" Royce sneered.

"Just that. I don't waste time on women."

"Women are a waste of time?"

"Yes, absolutely. They're whirlpools of need. They're parasitic. It's not their fault, really. They're wired that way."

"Wired? That's quite bold."

"Not really, it's self-evident."

"Ah, yes. Self-evident. Perhaps to you. But most of us aren't quite on your level. So just how is it self-evident?" Royce snapped, his face twisted in barely suppressed rage.

Strickland elaborated. Women, he explained, were subject to abuse by men because they were physically weaker. They also bared the burden of carrying children to term, a nine-month process during which they were particularly vulnerable. As a result, they sought out men for protection. It was adaptive behavior necessary for survival. But, over time, the same trait colonized their psyche, like cancer. Women's selfishness, therefore, was baked into the cake. "That's what I mean by wired."

I was bowled over by the audacious and grotesque argument. Strickland was cut from a different cloth, having quit a lucrative job for an uncertain future in art. That much was obvious. Yet I did not realize just how radical he was. He not only rejected the rat race, but also half the human race. What's more, he did so with such insouciance. He offered up his revolutionary ideas as though he were coldly reciting directions from an IKEA™ catalogue. It was breathtaking.

Royce slammed his fist down in anger. "This isn't a goddamned frat party," he yelled, even though such gatherings typically did approximate college bashes. "We can drop the infantile misogyny based on pseudoscience for which there is no evidence. It's embarrassing, like the sort of things teenagers say."

Others were intrigued, however, and implored Strickland to continue. "Ignore him," Alex cried out. "He's just upset because he's a kept man. Did I say that? I meant 'married' man. This hits too close to home." Alex mockingly gestured at Royce.

"Speaking of home, don't you have to go now? Isn't it past your wife's curfew?"

The place erupted in cheers and whistles.

Rob, a management consultant and father of two, with the ashen face of the overworked and upwardly mobile, penetrating green eyes, and curly hair, attempted to gain the floor through the din. Loosening his tie, as if readying for a brawl, he spoke loudly. "Hold on. Isn't it the case that women, not men, typically do most of the child-rearing? How then can you accuse women of self-centeredness? You've got things backward." He pointed at Strickland as he spoke. "It's women who are the prime givers, not men."

The room quieted. It was now a high-stakes volley, with each side blasting shots across the net in hopes of winning decisive rhetorical points.

"They do," Strickland responded. "I concede the point. Mothers mother far more than fathers father. It's undeniable. But complex motivations, not least the desire to propagate one's own genes, are at play. In this regard, child-rearing might be an expression of enlightened self-interest as much as selflessness, though the matter risks getting into another tangled discussion about the nature of generosity. Regardless, when it comes to their partners, women are single-mindedly out for protection and therefore in it for themselves."

Clapping erupted. Advantage Strickland.

"You've got things ass backward," snarled Royce.

"Not at all," responded Strickland. "My ass is riding in the right direction. That's the point. Women undermine that. Their neediness crowds out everything else. Being with a woman means sacrificing one's own ambition, one's sense of self. A relationship's whole, from a man's point of view, is less than the sum of its parts. It's the reverse for women."

"Hold on," Franklin said, gesturing for quiet. Pint-sized and unassuming, with a round face featuring a pair of plaintive eyes, Franklin hailed from a poor black Southern family only a few generations removed from sharecropping. He was an outlier. As a math teacher at a local magnet school, he was an island of altruism in the presence of a throng of corner-office executives in training. This gave him moral authority—in my eyes.

"Your argument," he said calmly, "is logically inconsistent. If women are selfish to the core, as you suggest, why do we seek them out? In every culture, we pursue them with reckless abandon. Why don't we realize the danger if it's as plain as you say?"

The room once again hushed.

Strickland smiled.

"That's clear. We're also wired—for sex. We'll do anything to get it. The hunt for carnal pleasure and associated competition between men to satisfy that primordial urge is what nine-tenths of all human affairs is about. Illogical? Not at all. It's nature's way of ensuring the survival of our species, as we likely would have little to do with women otherwise."

A rousing cheer erupted, as if Strickland, seemingly out of position, had managed to reach a well-placed passing shot and hammer one of his own.

"You can't be serious," snapped Royce. "What about companionship? What about love? Do these not figure into the equation? Apparently not. To you it just boils down to irredeemable selfishness on women's part and carnal instinct on ours. It's a dirty bargain: women pay for protection with their bodies. They're prostitutes, and we're gullible johns. It's as fucked up and simplistic as your commie ideas."

"I may be simplistic, but that's a simplification of my simplicity," replied Strickland, unruffled. "I wonder: if sex were taken out of the equation, would men have much to do with women? Would we seek out their company?"

Nobody answered.

Strickland continued. "We wouldn't, because women aren't interesting. This doesn't imply they're mentally deficient. Not in the least. Women are as smart as men. Probably smarter. They just don't use their minds. Women who do tend to hang out with men for this very reason. The opposite isn't true: men rarely socialize with women when the possibility of sex isn't in play.

"This is why the aging process is far more devastating to females, as they know that they offer little else besides their looks. Time may wait for no man, but it's particularly unforgiving for women."

"So women are selfish *and* dumb," Royce parried. "The indictment keeps growing."

"It's two sides to the same coin. Women are both selfish *and* incurious because they're consumed with seeking protection."

I was not convinced. Gita was narcissistic, but by no means did she require a guardian. On the contrary. She was self-sufficient and strong. She needed no one. That was the problem. If she actually wanted true companionship, then she would take an interest in my interests and explore what made me tick. But all that mattered to her was medicine and the prestige associated with it. Why, then, did I stay with her? One possibility at least partially did vindicate Strickland's twisted thesis: I was in it for the sex.

"That's crazy talk," Royce said with exasperation. "Even if

women are in fact 'consumed with protection' for reasons that go back to our earliest days as a species, and have this message encoded into their psyche, as you say, maybe they achieve the selfish ends through selfless means, like love and affection. If so, it's win-win: women get security, and we men get tenderness. What's wrong with that? That's a trade most guys would happily make! But for you, it's all give and take—we give and women take. There's no nuance. It's simple, straightforward...and crass. You're like a racist, Strickland, only worse. Instead of calling one racial group inferior, you're condemning half of humanity."

The room once again burst into hysterics.

"I had second thoughts about letting him in when he showed up in a white sheet and pointy hat," Alex added, prompting further laughter.

"Besides," Royce continued, "you've admitted that at least some women are interesting, so your argument is merely a generalization—and one lacking evidence. In actuality, everything you're saying is speculation—nothing more. It's not based on any evidence, just your own screwed-up ideas."

"Maybe you're right," Strickland countered. "But I think that's overstated. I heard about a recent study that found, for single guys, physical appearance was the biggest factor determining whether they reported a connection on a date. Single women, on the other hand, were more likely to believe a date was a success if they spent a good deal of time talking about themselves. So there you have it: guys are governed by their sex drive, while women prioritize guys' interest in *them*, which can be understood as an indicator of willingness to provide protection, since a male wouldn't put himself at risk for something he was apathetic about.

"But you've got a point, Royce. What I've said relates to most women, not all women. It's a matter of probability. Some July days are cold. Some birds can't fly. Some people in finance are smart…"

"Oh!" everyone groaned in delight at Strickland's takedown.

"Some women are giving," Strickland continued. "Some are curious. Some can even dunk a basketball. But most can't. It's a generalization, yes, but that hardly means it's wrong.

"Generalizations also apply to men. Lots of guys play video games, watch sports, and drink beer. They lack any smarts whatsoever. They're idiots. But others aren't."

"Well, I guess you're an equal-opportunity hater," Royce cried, eliciting a round of boos. Strickland clearly had the upper hand, but he went on anyway. "And being so enlightened about women's wily ways, you can't be bothered with them."

"Correct."

"You're on strike—on strike from women. And this is why you never leave your monastery or studio or whatever—is that right, Strickland?"

"That's part of it."

"You're too enlightened to have a sex drive. You're a monk, after all."

"Hardly," Strickland objected. "I just won't let it govern my life and ensure I make poor decisions."

"And how do you do that?"

"Not easily. It took a long time to figure out how. For years, I pursued women blindly. I was as much a hostage to my sex drive as anyone. I practically took every single woman in this town to dinner. I was a one-man food aid program. I could've advised the U.N. The one-way wooing grew tiring. I, as the man, *always* asked the women out. I, as the man, *always* drove the conversation at dinner. I, as the man, *always* paid the bill. If a second date was in the offing, it would only happen if I, as the man, suggested it. I was preacher and choir, teacher and student, doctor and patient—all because I was not in control. My sex drive was. I'm no victim. These are the rules to the game. There's no alternative if you want in—"

"And by 'in,' you mean that in a literal way," observed Royce crassly. Several people whistled loudly. Things were getting ugly. It was fantastic.

"Well, no, not intentionally. If you want sex, though, that's the price of admission. Which is why we guys—straight guys—put up with it. Women have the advantage because we're sex driven. As a result, guys eventually submit to nature's bargain: we agree to provide 'protection' in return for sex on demand. It's called marriage, and it's a lousy bargain."

Dammit, I thought, maybe he's got a point. My own carnal desires possibly had led me into oblivion. I had settled for a "relationship" with someone poorly suited for me because she was pretty. I got sex on demand—sometimes, at least—but not in exchange for protection, rather as recompense for self-absorption.

"I guess you're never getting hitched?" Royce asked acidly.

Strickland did not answer.

"So, you don't date, and marriage doesn't suit you. You reject both. Yet you claim that, even though you refuse to be 'governed' by your sex drive, it remains intact. What am I missing? How do you square that circle?"

"Cold showers?" added Alex, eliciting cheery amusement.

Strickland, composed as ever, smiled. "What's the secret of my success?"

"'Success' is one way of putting it," retorted Royce.

"You're asking how I satisfy my sex drive. That's what you

want to know? Well, there are 'friends with benefits.' There are casual hookups. There's porn…"

"Pathetic," Royce snarled.

"For you, maybe. And that's fine—to each his own. But no victory is cost-free, not least that over nature and its attempt to submit us to the female yoke. Such is the price of my victory."

"Victory?" uttered Royce.

"This doesn't mean I am not open to meeting a woman. Not at all. I'd love to love the right person. But that search occurs on my own terms, unencumbered by basic drives that cloud my judgment and, if unchecked, ensure submission."

"Submission?"

"Yes, submission to women's selfishness. I won't submit."

"You're talking to someone who wouldn't 'submit' to a high-paying job in finance," Alex chimed in, ribbing his childhood friend and stirring up the crowd. "The high-six-figure salary, the holiday bonus, the expense account, the car service, the four-star dinners—the indignity was too much for Strickland. He wouldn't submit. Not him!"

"A toast," Alex roared, holding aloft a can of beer. Everyone followed suit, even Royce, begrudgingly. "Here's to Strickland, a man on a mission of defiance. Voted into high office, he'll demand a recount; given the gift of gab, he'll remain mute; left a fortune, he'll turn it down.

"I don't understand you, my friend," he added, looking directly at Strickland. "You quit your job to pursue art, and you quit pursuing women because it's a job. Where others struggle to push boulders up hills, you fight to stop their downward momentum. I am at a total loss. I know you well, but I hardly know you. And yet I suspect that, in the end, you're going to be remembered, not any of us. Remembered for what, I'm not sure, but remembered all the same. To you, Strickland, whose only rule is to break all rules."

"To Strickland," everyone shouted. Royce stayed quiet.

85

CHAPTER 6

ABSURDIA

Guerillas had kidnapped another Westerner in the Philippines, demanding a ransom within forty-eight hours or their hostage, a Norwegian aid worker, would be killed. One of Marshland Cooper's biggest clients, an energy concern with plans to build power plants in the Philippines, was worried.

Mortimer's Saturday morning email requested immediate assistance drafting a report to lay out the pros and cons of the client's posture in the country. It was the sort of nonobligatory obligation that you could refuse in theory, but not in practice— like the Eco-Excellence campaign.

Putting in overtime was rare at Marshland Cooper, so I could not complain about the inconvenience. Yet, the previous night at Alex's had left me oddly befuddled and thus unable to fully concentrate on the task at hand. I had not drunk much, nor stayed particularly late. Still, I felt residual unease, though I did not know precisely why. It was like I had awoken anxiously from a disturbing dream whose exact details I could not recall.

This much was clear: I, like most of Alex's guests, had delighted in Strickland's epic rant and corresponding takedown of such an uptight snob as Royce. It was all good fun. Only Strickland was serious. His was not an act; he really believed what he was saying. What was more, his jaundiced view of women was only surpassed by his nonchalance about it. He was an emperor who cared not that he wore no clothes.

But why, then, was I bothered?

I pondered the matter without resolution. Seeking clarity, I gave Alex a call before departing for the office, but he was also on his way to work and therefore unable to chat. We made vague plans to rendezvous, which, given the demands of Alex's job, meant in weeks. And, so, I headed out for Marshall Cooper's Midtown office curiously out of sorts.

"Welcome to paradise," Brilliant Brad said when I arrived. "I've already been here four hours, and I stayed late yesterday, too."

"No man is indispensable," I replied, placing my wet umbrella in the corner of the lobby, "but you're an exception, which is why you're always first in and last out. You should be flattered. You're this place's backbone."

Brilliant Brad was unmoved. "Indispensable?" he asked skeptically, wiping his brow. "Yeah, right. You think I wouldn't be put out to pasture if prison laborers could do my job? Mortimer would give me black-and-white jammies as a parting gift to remind me that I'm not indispensable. No one is."

"You have a way of inspiring people," I responded, deadpan. "A real skill. Have you thought of going into motivational speaking?"

Brilliant Brad laughed. "I think you're on to something."

"You'd tank the whole economy with your demoralizing speeches," I joked. "We'd have another crisis."

Brilliant Brad's face fell. My ribbing had gone too far. "I'm just kidding," I said, backtracking. "You really are the backbone here. I'm serious."

"Shameless flattery will get you nowhere," Brilliant Brad replied.

Presently, the door to the conference room opened, and Mortimer and Marcy strode in together. They needed a signature song to accompany their entrance, like those played for baseball players when they come up to bat. An entire song wouldn't even be necessary. A few ominous notes would do, like the iconic refrain from Beethoven's Fifth Symphony. *Dah-dah-dah-dahhhh.* That would work. Mortimer was strangely attired in a blue-and-white seersucker suit, pink Oxford shirt, floral ascot, and black loafers worn without socks. He looked ready to take in a polo match or attend a midsummer soiree.

Marcy, by contrast, was dressed to the nines in a black business suit, purple blouse, and heels. A pen held her hair in a tight beehive. She looked ready for corporate battle.

"I'm glad you two are here," Mortimer announced. "We're expecting a few others: Claire, Pratyush, Margot, Lin, and...."

"Walter," Marcy added.

"Correct, Walter. So we've got solid representation, which I appreciate on such short notice. I wouldn't have interrupted your weekend were it not important. I myself just learned of the kidnapping earlier this morning from Oliver," he elaborated. "I initially thought we could observe events for a day or two, as these crises oftentimes are short-lived. That was the case when the South African mining strike hit the platinum sector last year, and during the wave of nationalization in Russia the year before, but you never really know. The only certainty is uncertainty. My inclination would be to sit tight for a few days to see how this plays out, since the rebels have promptly released hostages in the past. That could happen again. Oliver, however, called to say that Magellan's CEO rang him directly, seeking guidance.

"That's a testament to our reputational standing, of course, but that doesn't come for free. We've got to be on call when crises strike. Our clients expect as much. Which is why we're here today.

"I don't think it's worth going into great detail now about our work plan, since the others haven't showed up yet. Hopefully, they'll arrive soon, and when they do, we'll have an all-hands to bring everyone up to speed. For now, I'm going to leave you in Marcy's capable hands, as she's going to take over for the time being."

Mortimer then departed.

"Okay, let's get started," Marcy chirped insipidly, flipping her hair ostentatiously and adjusting her designer glasses. "So, as you've heard, there was another kidnapping in the Philippines. When Mortimer called me with the news this morning, I was like, Oh. My. God. I had a friend who went to Manila once, and I could only imagine what I'd do if she got abducted. I think I'd die.

Marcy then pivoted from Valley Girl to management maestro. "Anyway, we have to put together a time-sensitive piece on the Philippines' investment climate. Mortimer and I were thinking that it shouldn't be more than ten pages. Twelve, max. Okay, fifteen, counting appendixes.

"Speaking of the appendixes, Brad, you'll be responsible for them. We're looking for something snappy, something that gets to the heart of the matter. You know, maybe a few pie charts and bar graphs laying out level of foreign investment by year, market capitalization, and—well, you know, all that economic stuff.

"Liv, I want you to work on a short piece on security in the Philippines, especially the region where the kidnappings occurred. I forget its name. Mandingo or something. Whatever.

"So when I say short, I mean short—you have a tendency to draw things out too much. This isn't a thesis or dissertation. Just a page or so. Nothing more. Any questions? No? Okay, let's get started. We'll reconvene when everyone else shows up, but you can get underway in the interim."

Brad and I stood up without saying a word. "Oh, Liv, can you stay for a moment?" Marcy asked.

"Sure," I replied.

Marcy waited for Brilliant Brad to turn the corner before commencing. Leaning in, she said superciliously, "Liv, I see that you're not…well, how should I say it…performing very well in the Eco-Excellence campaign." She paused, perhaps hoping I might offer an explanation. I did not.

"The last time I checked, you were near the cellar, with just twenty-three points of excellence, nearly two hundred points off the lead. You haven't reported your weekly recycling activity for six weeks, nor have you opted in to the office's composting plan. You missed your rotation for turning off the lights at close of business—twice—and I heard you're even printing one-sided documents.

"I get the impression that you're not taking the initiative seriously, Liv, and I think that the campaign is mission-critical. By that I mean we both believe that it's an excellent opportunity to improve our environmental stewardship and, in so doing, build environmental consciousness in a way that will change our behavior permanently.

"Strictly speaking, it's voluntary. In that sense, the campaign isn't mission-critical. You're not obliged to participate; you won't be penalized if you don't. But we're really hoping that we'll get universal buy-in, as the values that the campaign embodies also embody Marshland Cooper's values, so in that way it is, well, critical. Does that make sense, Liv?"

Yet again, I conjured an excuse for my nonchalance about the campaign and assured Marcy, implausibly, that I would pay more attention. Placated, she trotted off, though not before flipping her hair dramatically.

Marcy personified the vacuity Strickland said allegedly afflicted the female gender. The likes of her normally would not have registered, as I would simply avoid someone so cloyingly shallow. But fate had swept me into Marcy's orbit, and I could not escape her gravitational pull. I was trapped.

Her transparent insincerity, glaring superficiality, and shameless vanity cut deep. What was glaringly obvious to me was not so to others, or at least not to those that "mattered" at work. Perhaps I was the fool, like the driver heading into oncoming traffic who, hearing an emergency radio announcement warning of a vehicle barreling down the wrong side of the road, says, "One vehicle? They're everywhere!"

I steadfastly refused to believe as much, given the implications of doing so. To question the fundamental perceptions that determine and underpin one's worldview is to question one's very grip on reality. A measure of faith that what we see is in fact what it is, therefore, is required for sustainable, ongoing sanity. Yet my doubts were growing. My world was overwhelmed by absurdity—an absurd job with absurd colleagues, an absurd relationship with an absurd girlfriend, an absurd political climate riddled by absurd blowhards—overwhelming my ability to cope. Marcy embodied a world gone mad.

For the moment, I had to suppress my anxiety, as well as my residual disquietude from the night before, and focus on the work at hand. I worked ably over the course of the next eight hours for our client, but the growing sense of weariness was increasingly difficult to suppress. In the past, it had come and gone, like a mirage on the desert, vanishing as suddenly as it had appeared. Now it emerged more frequently and with greater vibrancy.

What set it off, I did not know. It could have been Gita's self-indulgent complaining or the Comitan rally or Marcy's fatuous voice. It could have been boarding the congested subway during rush hour with a crush of other white-collared, robot-like professionals. It could have been Strickland's diatribe. Whatever the trigger, the suffocating feeling was sudden and overpowering.

My mounting anxiety prompted me to ramp up my gym regimen, as if fortifying my body would help me control my wayward mind. I also doubled down on meditation, regularly entering a trance-like state while conjuring myself at shore's edge on an isolated and pristine beach. Invariably, the recurring image of a wailing baby would rudely interrupt, yanking me out of my semiconscious state. And then there was the threatening steam engine haunting my dreams.

"Here we go again," Alex observed with a sigh when I confided my anxieties to him weeks later. "You're going psycho for no reason. Trust me. I've got a PhD in disappointment. I can identify real from imagined disillusionment, and you, my friend, have the latter. First, you've kept your job—and a good one at that—during a recession. What was that I saw in the paper yesterday? Oh yes, 'work is dignity.' The slogan was spray-painted in a slum. It's true. Work is dignity, and you have it."

I conceded the point. I had a solid job. There were far worse fates. But I had no passion for my work. And I hated office politics. I had left Washington in search of a "better" job, but I was back at square one. Different dog, same fleas.

Alex was not buying it. I sensed he was growing tired of my ennui. Nevertheless, he put on a brave face by recounting a safari he had taken to Africa. On the last day of his trip, he had gotten caught in traffic on the way to the airport. As night fell, a crush of humanity had emerged from the shadows "as if someone had pulled a fire alarm."

At first, he had been frightened by the chaos engulfing the road. But by then he had become reflective. Undoubtedly, the people outside the taxi were poor, but were they miserable? He was sure they were—at first. But he had second thoughts. "Their life experience, like mine, was full of the same emotions—joy, pain, anger, love, and so on. The context in which they experienced them was just different."

I offered up a skeptical look. A Wall Street investment banker actually was arguing that his life was no better than poor Africans. That was a first.

"No, really, I'm serious," Alex pleaded. "I'm not romanticizing things. Poverty is not fun. I get that. But they weren't starving, just poor. Okay, more than poor. People in the South Bronx are poor. Still, they probably weren't that different than you and me, regardless. It was like…" Alex's voice trailed off as he tried to conjure the right metaphor. "Like they were playing the same tune but several octaves lower."

"What?" I replied in disbelief. "Are you insane? You realize how that sounds? You do, I hope."

Alex waved me off. "Here's the deal: they might've even been happier than you or me. Yeah, it sounds crazy, I know, but it struck me that when you're living on a razor's edge, you don't have time for existential bullshit. 'Does my life have meaning?' 'What's my legacy?' All that handwringing is an unaffordable luxury, and that's probably a good thing.

"We get wrapped up in self-actualization crap because we can. We don't have real worries to concern ourselves with, at least not those faced by a lot of people on this planet. What I'm saying…"

"Yes, what are you saying, Alex?"

"What I'm saying is that, as your friend, I'd prescribe perspective."

Setting aside his claims about his life being no happier than those in seriously humbling circumstances, comparing my woes to far graver ones faced by others seemed unfair. I was not arguing I had it worse than most. Clearly that was not the case. But I did not think this forfeited my right to reflect on my situation. "Yes, everything is relative," I conceded. "Our lives compared with most are unfathomably good. But life isn't lived relatively. We compare ourselves to the surroundings and circumstances we know, not the ones we don't."

Alex was unconvinced. He suggested I take a step back from time to time. I might realize the world's weight wasn't on my shoulders by doing so. I turned the tables. Did he practice what he preached? Did he have perspective? If so, did that explain why he was in finance, an industry he loathed? "Well, I wouldn't say 'loathe,' but yes," he replied.

"Or maybe you're just justifying the unjustifiable." I was out for blood. If Alex alleged I was consumed by self-pity, I would point out the hypocrisy of his working in an industry about whose harm he was well aware. Two could play that game.

"Sure," Alex said, shrugging. "I could copy Strickland—"

"Strickland!" I interjected, my attention suddenly shifting to Alex's enigmatic friend. "I wanted to ask you about him. Is he for real? I mean, was he just fucking with Royce that night?"

Alex leaned back in his chair and inhaled deeply, stretching his long arms skyward as if in search of otherworldly inspiration. "I have no idea. I've known Strickland since we were kids and still can't figure him out. I was aware he didn't like his job, but not enough to quit. I couldn't believe it. I still can't. He's obviously got artistic talent, but it seems all so rash, or worse."

"And that bit about going on strike?"

"You mean his not dating?" Alex asked.

I nodded.

"Yeah, it's true. He thinks women are a waste of time in the same way he thought his job at the bank was a waste of time. So he quit both. I sort of admire him for it. Maybe you could take a cue from him."

I was taken aback. "You mean quit my job?"

"No, I was referencing quitting your girlfriend. You could do a lot better. Come to think of it, though, yeah, your job, too. I mean, I don't advise it. Like I said, I'd prescribe perspective—you know, Holocaust films, homeless shelters, and all that. But since you've been complaining so long about your job, why don't you pull a Strickland and just quit?"

"Why don't you?" I shot back, reverting to my earlier theme about his amoral job.

"It has crossed my mind. But I'm good at two things in this

world: crunching numbers and surfing. The latter doesn't pay, and the former does. I'm stuck. I'm an investment banker, Liv. I know you think I'm some cretin—"

"Yup, I do," I joked. Or maybe I wasn't kidding. I didn't know myself.

"Whatever. I'm not doing God's work, but I'm not cut out for much else. My plan is to stick with finance for a while, make a killing, hopefully without doing too much harm, and get out. Easy peasy."

"That's what they all say. You'll probably have a heart attack at your desk at fifty like all the rest. You'll be the richest man in the graveyard."

"Don't worry," Alex replied, "I'll put you in my will, 'cause I know when I die, whenever that may be, you'll still be at your job, wretched and miserable."

"Touché."

"Seriously, Liv, pull a Strickland. You like writing, no? Take a sabbatical to…"

"Pursue my passion?" I interjected ironically.

"Well, yeah. It's sort of cliché, but why not? Find out what it is that makes you *you*, and then go for it. For me, it's a future without having to work whatsoever. Your task is to find your passion. Don't you like writing?"

"I do, but don't have the nerve. Besides, I don't know what I'd do. I'm not like Strickland. I don't have some hidden talent. Certainly not writing. I'm good with languages, though. I picked up Spanish easily in college. That helps me how?"

"It's a start."

"I guess I'll have to rethink this humility thing."

"You mean perspective thing," Alex said.

"Yeah, whatever. Humility. Perspective."

"Bravo," Alex replied with a round of applause. "And while you're at it, dump Gita."

CHAPTER 7

THE BREAK

was unfolding my umbrella when a blow from a heavy fist, like a sock full of pennies, landed just below my left eye. I staggered backward, my head heavy and disoriented, before regaining my balance and wheeling around to identify the fist's owner: a Comitan.

It was my own fault.

I had overslept on account of an anxious night trying to outrun the onrushing steam engine, making me late for work. As I'd double-timed it out of the subway, I had taken little notice of the commotion between a half-dozen Comitans and some counterdemonstrators. Had I been more alert, I would have given the scuffling adversaries wide berth. But I was preoccupied and paid the price when a roundhouse intended for a long-haired man wearing a black shirt with an anarchist insignia crashed down on me instead.

"What the fuck?" I snapped at the Comitan, a tall, sinewy fellow approximately forty years of age. He had belligerent black eyes and a scraggly beard, and wore torn jeans and a shirt with the silhouette of a motorcycle. Initially, he seemed just as surprised as I by his errant blow, at least until my reaction set him off.

"Fuck you, too," he shot back. "Watch where you're going."

"Me?" I responded in disbelief. My eye would surely ripen into bright reds and yellows. "What did I do to you? I'm going to work. You know, to be productive. You should do the same."

Just then, three policemen arrived on scene. Several witnesses identified the Comitan as the instigator, prompting the cops to approach the aggressive malcontent.

"Yeah, that's the guy," I said. "He hit me."

"I hit who?" the Comitan responded irately. "The fucker's lying!"

Before I could respond, a Good Samaritan in a yellow rain jacket interjected. "I saw everything. That guy," he said, pointing to the Comitan, "punched him. I saw it."

"Is that true?" one of the officers asked the Comitan.

"No. Well, not intentionally. Okay, intentionally. That's right. I admit it. He fucking deserved it anyway. Look at him. He's just like the rest, with his business suit and arrogant—"

"I'm going to have to ask you to come with me," one of the officers said. "Please place your hands behind your back."

The Comitan stood motionless, apparently in disbelief. He then pointed an accusatory finger at me and yelled, "Fuck you, asshole."

With that the cops moved in, only to face resistance from the Comitan, who put up a fight, shoving one of the policemen back when he tried to cuff him. Two others set on the Comitan, wrestling him down and corralling his wrists behind his back. While writhing on the ground, the Comitan looked up at me and, through gritted teeth, groaned, "Fuckin' Jew."

I arrived to work twenty minutes late. I had just set down my briefcase and turned on my computer when Mortimer appeared. "Good morning, Liv," he said with a sunny countenance before spotting the growing welt on my face. "Dear me. What happened to you?"

"I got into a fight on the way to work," I replied.

"Are rush hours getting that unruly?"

"No, not really," I responded, before relaying the details of my unfortunate encounter.

"I'm so sorry," Mortimer replied sincerely. "I trust you don't need to go to the ER, as it looks rather superficial. You should put ice on it, though. You're welcome to leave a bit early if you'd like. Really, do go home once you've taken care of the essentials. Anyway, I apologize for the poor timing, given that you've just had a bit of a dustup, but I wanted to chat with you for a moment. We're going to reorganize things around the office. I've done a lot of thinking of late, and I believe we need a course correction. Nothing too dramatic, I dare say, but a reorienting of the ship to ensure smoother sailing ahead. Later in the week, we'll be having a staff meeting where things will be fully fleshed out, but for now I thought it was important to briefly touch base with everyone in person to nip any rumors in the bud.

"The long and short is that we're going to alter our organizational structure to better deliver solutions to our clients. This means we are going to move away from team structures built around subject-matter expertise to ones with a geographical focus, with Doug and Pratyush taking overall responsibility for the office's day-to-day operations. They'll serve as my deputies, formalizing the arrangement as it effectively stands now. You, Brad, Mark, and Ayesha will form a team working under Marcy's authority. She'll serve as team lead. We'll discuss this in more detail on Thursday, but I wanted you to hear it from me first. Regardless, I think this is going to be an exciting time here. We're going to be postured to bravely chart ahead. For now, Liv, don't hesitate to leave early, as you're surely a bit out of sorts, given your unfortunate encounter."

Mortimer turned to leave and had taken two steps toward his own office when he pivoted. "Oh, Liv," he said, "I see that you're still a bringing up the rear in the Eco-Excellence campaign. You know you're risking relegation. You know about relegation, don't you?"

I did, but he explained anyway.

"In English, the weakest clubs at year's end are downgraded a division. Right now, you're dangerously close to relegation." He laughed. "Oh, I'm just kidding. We don't operate that way." He slapped my back and trotted off.

Inner turmoil can build over time before it ruptures spectacularly, like the sudden shifting of tectonic plates, bursting through the fetters once holding it in check. The proximate cause of my own emotional earthquake was a one-two punch: the first was a literal blow, courtesy of the Comitan; the second, a metaphorical blow—Mortimer's announcement that I would be reporting directly to Marcy.

I'd been unhappy for years but done nothing. Now, in a single moment, Mortimer had provided the perfect trigger. The moment he disappeared from view, I resolved to quit my job.

The decision was both sudden and final. A feeling of weightlessness came over me instantly, despite all the insecurity I knew would follow. I felt unburdened, free. I was no longer a kept man.

I tendered my resignation at week's end, just after the office-wide meeting formalizing the office reorganization.

"I hope it had nothing to do with that relegation comment," Mortimer said, almost defensively. "You know that was a joke. We really value your work here and are sad to see you go."

I fabricated a story about receiving a few offers from firms on the West Coast. This would fulfill, I said apocryphally, a long-standing ambition to move to California. The ruse worked. And by good fortune, Marcy happened to be out of the office for my final two weeks, thereby permitting my escape without any awkward goodbyes.

On my last day, Brilliant Brad dropped by my cubicle and asked some probing questions about my future plans. I deftly parried his inquiries but stumbled when he asked the names of my potential employers. "I don't want to say until I've finally accepted one of their offers," I replied. "It wouldn't feel right."

Brilliant Brad did not buy it. I could tell. "Well, good luck with everything," he said, shaking my hand goodbye. "I admire what you're doing."

"That was very sudden," my mother remarked when I broke the news. Her tone was neutral, neither condemning nor condoning, as if she had no stake in the matter, which in fact she did not. "The apple doesn't fall far from the tree," she added matter-of-factly. "What will you do now?"

I told her I planned to move to Spain. "With the savings I've put away, plus the monies Granny left me, I could probably live a year with no income, possibly more. I'll be able to improve my Spanish, which is rusty, and more importantly, I'll be able to figure out what I want to do next."

My mother pondered the matter for a few moments. "It might

be hard to get back in the game once you've taken yourself out. Not that I'm one to talk. You father and I have always marched to our own drummer, and so I could hardly fault you for doing the same."

With that she changed direction. "Speaking of which, Liv, we do love it here in Southern California," she said, her tone upbeat. "I must confess that some of it has to do with the climate. I do not miss those Midwest winters. You adapt this sort of bunker mentality when you're in the thick of it. It's only when you're removed from it that you see how injurious it really is. Not that I regret our time in Wisconsin. Hardly. It was a period of great growth."

My mother went on a customary tangent about herself and her undiminished quest for self-actualization. The monologue might have set a personal record for longevity had my father not interrupted. "Oh, Liv, I'm sorry, your father just got back from work and wants to talk to you. I'll have to tell you the rest later. There's so much to say."

My father was more suspicious about my plans. "The economy isn't good," he reminded me. "The worst of the crisis may be behind us, but we're still in a very rough patch. And even though you've got solid credentials, it may not be easy to find something else. Why don't you hold off leaving until you find another job? That sounds like the wise thing to do."

He counseled me to remain in New York before departing for Spain, though he expressed sympathy when I articulated the depth of my despair on the corporate treadmill.

"It's risky, Liv," he said. "Very risky. Now's not the time to jump into the unknown. In fact, you couldn't have picked a worse time. I would counsel patience."

I understood my father's advice came from the heart. He

only wanted what was best for me. The same also was true of my mother, her boundless narcissism notwithstanding. Yet they both spoke from an emotional remove that failed to consider matters from my point of view. They lacked empathy. This was no lament. In this my mother and father were hardly alone; in fact, I think parental obliviousness to the inner lives of their children is the norm, even in close-knit families.

Take Alex, who was very tight with his parents, whom he visited as often as possible, given his busy work schedule. He spoke of them as loving caretakers during his childhood, taking great interest in his life and that of his younger sister. And yet they knew nothing about his aspirations to someday quit a job he believed had no redeeming value. It was not something he shared with them, despite its significance.

We all have personas tailored to specific audiences and settings. For Alex, the one he deployed around his parents, for whatever reason, had certain restrictions, at least as it pertained to his ambitions. His mother and father therefore were ignorant about an important part of his character, an essence of who he was. They were not privy. In this particular way, Alex might have been unusual. But everyone has multiple personas, some of which inevitably remain hidden at any given time, including to one's family, no matter how close relations might be.

For this reason, I never gave too much thought to my parents' lack of understanding about me or the more genuine persona they never saw. Since I chose not to share it with them, I could hardly complain about their being in the dark. They had their lives and I had mine. It was a good bargain, as far as I was concerned. It gave me freedom, liberating me from oppressive expectations—theirs and mine.

Nevertheless, informing my parents of my decision was difficult. I know they worry about me—not a lot, but somewhat. I felt bad for burdening them; they already have enough on their minds, themselves. Telling Gita would be far worse, though not because she would be hurt by my sudden departure, thereby effectively ending our relationship, or even shocked by it. She, like my parents, had little understanding of what drove me, but unlike them, she viewed with disdain that which she did not understand. A deep reservoir of contempt lay beneath.

I cannot blame her entirely. We're both at fault. A desultory relationship suited our needs for the time being, yet mutual resentment borne from our fundamental incompatibility simmers below the surface, ready to erupt at the slightest provocation. It's the downside of being coldly opportunistic when it comes to romance. What you put in is what you get out. A messy rupture was inevitable.

I tried reaching Gita repeatedly the night I gave notice, but she kept brushing me off on account of her work schedule. "I can't talk," she snapped one evening when I rang. "Livie, I work hard," implying I did not. A few days later, she finally agreed to carve out some time between shifts when I said I needed to see her urgently. We linked up at her hospital's cafeteria.

"What's all the fuss, Livie?" she asked when we finally met. "You know how busy I am." She adjusted her scrubs' drawstring. "I can't be at your beck and call. You just don't understand how busy a doctor's life is. Today I did rounds with this stand-in attending who was a total tyrant. After every patient we saw, he would explain why he'd done this or that and why his was the only way. For the last two patients, he had me take the lead. One, an elderly woman with a broken pelvis, was in a morphine-induced daze, and the other, a middle-aged man who had had a motorcycle accident, who also was barely communicative. But the attending said I messed things up with both. I didn't 'engage them effectively.' Seriously? They were basically comatose!"

"Liv, this is the crap I have to put up with. You just don't get it. I mean, your job isn't…it just isn't the same. You don't understand," she repeated with exasperation. "Anyway, what do you want to talk about so badly? What's so important?"

"Well, it is important." I got right to the point. "I quit my job."

"Oh." She reacted with confusion. "Did you get another one?"

"No."

Gita shook her head in disapproval. "Oh, Livie," she sighed, rubbing her forehead. "I don't even want to know. I've never understood your decision-making anyway. You're lost to this world. What are you going to do?"

"I'm going to Spain."

"For how long?"

"I'm not sure," I answered.

"What do you mean, 'not sure'?" Gita replied with a huff.

"I have no idea."

"This is a vacation?"

"Not really. I'm flying out at the end of the month. I could be gone for six months, but it could be for a while longer."

Gita stared at me blankly. Undoing her bun, she ran her hand through her matted hair. Exhaling deeply, she asked in disbelief, "You're quitting your job and moving to Spain? That's your plan?"

"Yup."

Gita said nothing. Momentarily, I thought she might be composing herself as the shock of our relationship's demise sunk in. Even placeholders biding time can develop affection. I contemplated embracing her or perhaps reaching for her hand. But I had misjudged things. Gita's expression transformed from one of confusion to disdain. "Look, Livie," she snarled, "it's your life. You can make your own decisions. But I don't get how a grown man—you're going to be thirty soon—acts like a child. Who quits their job without finding another one and just moves abroad? That's so irresponsible. I'd expect more from my teenage niece!"

"I didn't think you'd understand," I replied.

"Understand? What's there to understand? What you're doing is reckless. Stupid. Dumb. You have no plan. And don't think this is about me. Or us. It's not. I mean, I don't mean to be blunt, but it's not like we'll all that serious. We're not. Never were. We were just, well, convenient. I know that sounds mean, but it's true. We both know it.

"Anyway, it's your life. If you want to screw it up, that's on you, but don't expect me to understand. I'm an adult. Lives depend on me—literally. I have responsibilities, Liv," she added, switching to a more formal diminutive. "Responsibility may be a foreign concept to you, but not to the rest of us in the *real* world."

"Yes, you're responsible. You work hard. I admire that. But…"

I struggled for words. Happily cloistered and living a conventional and altogether blinkered existence, Gita's worldview was liberating. She was blissfully ignorant, protected from the intellectual and emotional preoccupations, concerns, and ills that dogged others, especially me. She didn't know what she didn't know, nor did she care. Such was her freedom.

Gita's myopia was never tested because she was a "success." She had the right degrees from the right schools, she had a budding career in medicine, and she was ensured a lucrative paycheck in due course. She had done things right by the standards that mattered. Why, then, fix what was not broken?

For Gita, my search for meaning was a mysterious ailment reflecting some peculiar pathology, as was my odd fixation with matters that were neither important nor within my grasp to affect, like current events. It spoke to an alarmingly deviant value system that rejected the conventional values she held dear. There was something wrong with me. I had gone rogue. Thus, attempting to explain myself was akin to describing the majesty of color to the blind or the beauty of poetry to the stonehearted. No words would do. We spoke no common tongue.

"But what?" Gita asked impatiently.

"Look, you've found a job you like. You're happy with it. You're satisfied. That's fantastic…"

"So this is all about not liking your job? Lots of people don't. You think I like being treated like crap by my attending? But few quit on a moment's notice and run away."

"It's not just about my job."

"Then what is it, Liv?"

"Yes, my job stinks, but it's more than that. It's the state of the country, too. Earlier this week, in fact, a Comitan punched me in the face." I pointed to my left eye.

"A Comitan? What are you talking about?" She was becoming exasperated and clearly didn't recall our encounter with the noisy misfits at Columbus Circle. "Look," she added, her patience exhausted, "I have no idea what you're talking about, nor, frankly, do I care. This has nothing to with us. There never really was an us. We both know that. It's about you—your immaturity. I say that without anger. It's an honest assessment. Regardless, I hope your find what you're looking for, Liv, whatever that may be. I really do. You're not a bad person. You're just a child—a man-child.

"I live in a different world...with responsibilities, a world where patients depend on me. I mean *really* depend on me. It's a world of hopes, ambitions, and goals. It's a world with direction. It's an adult world."

"Fine," I said, realizing the conversation's futility. "I know I shouldn't have just sprung this on you. Even if there never was an us, we've still been seeing each other, or whatever you want to call it. You had the right to know that I was leaving, not just learn about it after the fact. I'm sorry, Gita."

"There's no need to apologize," she replied coldly. "I'm not hurt. We both know we're not right for each other. That was clear from the get-go. We fit into each other lives for the time being. That's it. This isn't about us. It's about you. As an impartial ob-server—and I mean that—what you're doing is self-destructive. You're just running away from your problems. But your problems relate to your own irresponsibility, so you can't run away from them. I'll be fine. It's *you* that you have to worry about. But you'll learn eventually." Her shook her head in exasperation, as though I had claimed to have been the victim of an alien abduction. I was lost to the world in her eyes.

"I'm glad you understand," I responded acidly.

Gita stood up and gave me a halfhearted hug. "Best of luck, Liv. I really hope you find what you're looking for. I mean it, I do." She then turned and disappeared around the corner.

Three weeks later, on a stormy evening, I departed for Spain. While waiting for my flight, moments from finally bidding fare-well to New York and all its unpleasant associations in my life, I suddenly was gripped by a foreboding sense of doubt. I anxiously thought about what I could have done differently. Should I have stayed at my job in Washington? Steady government work has its virtues. Perhaps I had had unreasonable expectations, ensuring that I would be disappointed at Marshall Cooper, or anywhere. Maybe Alex was right, I needed perspective—and not just about my career. Modesty might be in order.

As I sat in nervous contemplation, a crowd gathering beneath a television caught my attention. Edward Schmidt, the prominent right-wing radio personality—whose electrifying speech at a gun rights convention in Dallas a year earlier—had just announced he would be running for president. "We're going to take this country back," he promised rapt supporters in Virginia, "and make America great again!"

I boarded minutes later.

PART II

DAWN

CHAPTER 8

INTO THE VOID

The radiant Mediterranean sun enveloped me as I exited the terminal at Barcelona's main airport. Pulling down the brim of my Detroit Tigers cap to shield the glare, I walked woozily toward a queue for a city-bound bus. I had two large valises containing the sum total of my life's possessions in tow and reality set in.

The die was cast.

A few dozen bystanders speaking an array of undecipherable languages were lined up under an awning, forcing me to loiter in the unforgiving sun. Even though it was a brisk autumn day, beads of sweat formed a channel and cascaded down my back, turning my shirt sticky, like wet papier-mâché. I felt hot and cold all at once.

When the bus finally emerged, a sullen-faced driver exited, lit a cigarette, and announced in thickly accented English, "Sixteen euro. Sixteen. One way. No two way. One way. Sixteen euro."

I heaved my two valises into the undercarriage and handed the driver damp currency that I had been clutching in my perspiring palm. I climbed aboard. Minutes later we were on the move.

My head leaned between the seat back and window as, fighting exhaustion, I took in the scenery. Spain's rugged terrain, though hardly lush, was not as parched and arid as I had imagined. In undeveloped expanses, the ground was dotted with squat trees and thatch-like underbrush, resembling a desert's edge, over the horizon of which the craggy vegetation might give way to sand dunes.

As we neared Barcelona's periphery, austere apartment blocks and large box stores announced themselves, and the city's iconic yellow-and-black-painted taxis became abundant. I wondered why Barcelona was so famed for its beauty.

As we drove on, however, the architecture grew more impressive. Entering the city center itself, elegant buildings began to dot the cityscape. The buildings featured steel, glass, bricks, and ceramics and incorporated symbols of Catalan identity like Saint George of dragon-slaying lore. The striking architecture sharply contrasted with New York's glass-curtain towers that prioritize functionality over aesthetics, reflecting a stultifying corporate ethos.

The bus made two more stops before reaching our ultimate destination, the Plaça de Catalunya, a sprawling expanse in the city's heart. "Okay, everyone," the bus driver announced when we arrived, "we are here. You leave now."

I retrieved my luggage and oriented myself toward La Rambla, the tree-lined thoroughfare that twisted nearly a mile from the Plaça de Catalunya to a monument of Columbus near the water's edge. Its spine, running between two lanes of traffic, served as a pedestrian mall and teemed with performance artists, kiosks, and cafés.

I walked down the boulevard, stopping briefly to watch a

magician and then a jazz quartet, while keeping close track of the cross streets. Three street-theater acts later, near where a dozen African immigrants were selling illegal knockoff purses, I spotted my rendezvous point.

A woman waved as I approached. It was Anna—whose sister Marta, along with her husband Aitor, owned the apartment I'd found online. She was about sixty, skinny and short. Her blond hair was cut in a bob framing her long, narrow face, which featured a striking pair of large brown eyes that reflected inner intelligence and complexity. Smiling warmly, she was dressed in a pair of jeans, a sweater, and canvas sneakers.

"Liv?" she asked, pronouncing my name correctly.

"*Sí, soy* Liv," I responded affirmatively in the first Spanish I had spoken since taking a vacation to Costa Rica several years earlier.

Anna leaned in and kissed me on both cheeks, the customary Spanish greeting. I was nevertheless taken aback by the warm gesture, a reaction that gave Anna pause. She blanched slightly, apparently embarrassed on my behalf. I apologized, explaining in broken Spanish that Americans are reserved.

"Bueno," Anna answered with a chuckle, "tendremos que cambiar eso. Ven, déjame llevarte a tu nuevo lugar." (*We'll have to change that. Come, let me take you to your new place.*)

She gestured in the opposite direction. "You'll have time to tell me about your trip on the way. I'm sure you're very tired."

As we wended our way through the labyrinthine streets of the Barri Gòtic (the Gothic Quarter), abutting the Rambla, Anna asked what brought me to Barcelona. Succinctly explaining my decision would have been a challenge in English, much less in Spanish. Moreover, my American accent was grating, even to my own ears. After several false starts, I put it simply. "I just needed a change."

Anna kindly assumed responsibility for the conversation. Playing tour guide, she pointed out the historical significance of churches, plazas, and other landmarks in the medieval quarter, some of which dated to Roman times.

The mental exertion required to follow Anna's thread, even though she had slowed her cadence, took its toll. My brain worked feverishly to keep pace, requiring real-time translation from Spanish to English. It was like mentally arranging fridge-magnet word fragments in one language to form coherent sentences in another, only to reverse the process to articulate thoughts. The effort was quickly sapping my remaining energy.

After passing a quaint plaza where café patrons were chatting amiably, Anna pointed in the direction of a modest apartment building whose sand-colored facade was blackened with soot. Despite its shop-worn exterior, charming balconies with flowers and the occasional Catalan independence flag—horizontal red and yellow stripes emanating left to right from a blue triangle with a white star in its middle—gave it a certain weathered elegance.

As we approached a wooden door suited for a medieval castle, Anna announced, "*Estamos aquí.*" We had arrived. From her pocket, she produced an elaborate key with numerous grooves and ridges and inserted it into the lock. With three firm twists to the left, the latch clicked and Anna pushed open the heavy door to reveal a crypt-like vestibule—cavernous and dark. A single overhead bulb, which came on when the door opened, dimly lit the mysterious recesses.

Anna motioned toward a twisting staircase assembled with irregular stone steps. Tenuously hoisting my valises, I followed her up two flights to a modest landing that had a single rust-colored door. "This is your new home," Anna said in Spanish.

She produced another key, only slightly less elaborate than the first, and opened the door, beckoning me inside. The modern apartment, true to its appearance online, was wholly incongruous with the unloved building. The large living area was tastefully decorated with a fashionable leather couch, glass table, and large flat-screen television. Impressionist reproductions dotted the room's freshly painted walls. To the right was an airy and bright kitchen with a large window facing the plaza, modern appliances and marble countertops. The one bedroom, by contrast, was windowless and dark but nevertheless attractively apportioned. The large bed in the center of the room was covered by a floral eiderdown that matched the rug. There was a metal dresser and lamps with colorful shades. The bathroom off the bedroom featured a walk-in tiled shower and sink whose basin was made of marble. Charming etchings of Barcelona landmarks hung on the walls.

"It's precious," I remarked.

"Yes, it is. My family bought it many years ago, a few years after the transition," Anna said, referencing the country's emergence from fascism to democracy in the mid-1970s. "It was run down then. The city was very different. This area was seedy, full of drug dealers and prostitutes. You wouldn't have wanted to be caught here at night. Friends pleaded with us not to purchase the place, but it was all my family could afford at the time. But it was the right choice."

I replied that I found it hard to believe the Gothic Quarter had ever fallen into disrepair, since it was so captivating and historic.

Anna was adamant. "It's true. Barcelona took off after the '92

Olympics. The Rambla transformed and so did the Barri—and not all for the better. Before it had character. The boutiques were unique. Now you get all the same chain stores. I suppose that's the price of progress. You'll notice signs demanding tourists leave. Don't pay them any attention. The city's fate is tied to foreign visitors, who drive the economy. The sentiment comes from a good place. Barcelona's unique character is threatened. It's becoming Disneyland."

Anna apologized for her digression before familiarizing me with the apartment's idiosyncrasies, such as the European washing machine that doubled as a dryer and iron radiators that clanged like a "percussion section" as they warmed up. When I yawned inadvertently, Anna suggested she get on her way. "You'll have a lot of time to take all this in, but for now it looks like you could use a nap. Don't sleep too long, or you won't be able to get to bed tonight."

I accompanied Anna out, at which point she gave me a hug and urged me to reach out if necessary. "It's not easy being a stranger in a strange place, so don't hesitate to call if you need anything."

I returned to the apartment and sat on the couch, taking in my new place. Once again, a foreboding sense of anxiety suddenly overcame me, as it had in the airport in New York. I felt jittery and hot, but the sensation soon passed. My eyelids then grew heavy, and I dozed off in a sitting position. I woke hours later to the sound of voices in the stairwell. The apartment was dark, save for a sliver of light from a streetlamp, emanating from a crack in the terrace shutters.

I roused myself and, without undressing, retreated to the bedroom and fell back asleep. As had occurred so many times before, I was transported to a high desert plain. Sweating beneath an unforgiving sun, I heard the whistle of a train resonating in the distance. The dream unfolded predictably, again confronting me with the impossible choice of whether to jump off the cliff or be crushed by the oncoming steam engine. As ever, I was paralyzed with indecision. My quandary had followed me uninterrupted across continents to remind me that escape was an illusion. Unless, of course, it was a premonition.

In the early hours of the morning, I woke and lay in bed lost in thought for some time, hoping to fall back asleep until daybreak. An hour passed. Eventually, I retrieved a travel guide to Barcelona from my backpack, as I figured I might as well see the sights.

When slivers of sunlight began to emerge through the crack in the balcony shutter, I climbed out of bed, showered, and dressed. Making sure to take my guidebook and collection of skeleton keys, I shuffled down the two flights of uneven stairs and emerged in the plaza with renewed vigor resulting from my resolution to escape my escape.

Wandering the Gothic Quarter aimlessly, I happened upon a small pastry shop that had just opened, with waiters still setting up small tables under the establishment's awning. I sat down and ordered *churros con chocolate*, a guidebook recommendation that comprised sticks of fried dough-like pastry speckled with sugar and a thick confection of chocolate for dipping purposes. I devoured the tasty treat.

"How did you like your churros?" my waiter asked in Eastern European–accented English when I finished.

"Is my Spanish that bad?" I responded sorrowfully.

"Well, no," he answered, "but I can tell you're not from here."

"Neither are you," I said.

Józef, tall and skinny, with large hazel eyes and ready smile, hailed from Kraków, Poland. He had moved to Spain, he said, roughly a year ago after completing college. "I had romantic images of the country. I read about the bullfighting and all. I had to come."

We carried on a pleasant conversation in English, much to my chagrin. My Spanish, even at its apex, was respectable at best, but it was also horrifyingly rusty. Nevertheless, I was ashamed that a foreigner had so readily identified me as a linguistically challenged comrade in arms.

When I mentioned I had just arrived in country, Józef recommended a language school. "Vive offers classes for all levels. It's not expensive, and the teachers are excellent. And it's not far from here—only a few blocks, in fact." I thanked him and thought nothing more of it.

Afterward, I retraced the route that Anna and I had taken the day before, making my way out of the Gothic Quarter back to the Rambla, which was a busy blur, even at this early hour, and then to the Plaça de Catalunya, where I bought a ticket on a hop-on, hop-off bus for tourists. As the first bus would not depart for another forty-five minutes, I took a casual walk around the plaza that had once sat outside the city's walls but had become the epicenter of the city after the battlements were removed in the nineteenth century.

The city's other famous thoroughfare, the Passeig de Gràcia, emanated from the Plaza. It was surrounded by hotels, banks, and retail establishments, the most famous of which, el Corte Inglés, a massive department store, resided in an iconic sand-colored, wedge-shaped building resembling an engine locomotive.

The plaza itself occupied an impressive expanse replete with fountains, sculpture, and monuments—and countless pigeons. Perhaps most striking to the foreign eye were its two marble female nudes, one squatting, her face resting contemplatively on a bended elbow, and the other situated between flowers and a fountain, arms crossed above her head, a drape falling by her waist.

Such public art might well have been scandalous in the U.S., but here in the cradle of Western civilization, where Christian denominations sometimes comprised the state religion, nude public art was part of the scenery. On this day, children were playing near the erotic sculpture. Only a pair of tourists from Asia, perhaps titillated, seemed to take any interest in them, snapping a few photographs. The more common reaction was indifference.

The tourist bus, a red double-decker resembling those found in London, eventually pulled into the far end of the plaza across el Corte Inglés, where other early-rising tourists formed a line. I boarded the vehicle and listened to a recorded narrative through headphones as we headed in the opposite direction of the Rambla toward the bohemian Gràcia neighborhood and the Parc Güell.

Like many of Barcelona's most iconic places, the Parc was designed by Antoni Gaudí, the sublimely creative Catalan architect whose enchanting work incorporated organic elements and themes as well as religious iconography. His work often featured an array of materials like ceramics, ironwork, and stained glass. Originally commissioned by a count to be a garden city for well-to-do Catalans seeking solace from urban hustle and bustle, the sprawling hilltop sanctuary had been a commercial failure. Ultimately, the estate was sold to the city and turned into a public venue, though not before Gaudí had left his unique mark on it. An indication of the Parc's magnificent eccentricity greeted ticketed visitors at the park's main entrance. In the middle of a fountain stood guard what appeared to be a large, multicolored, mosaic, salamander-like creature, its mouth agape. It was actually a dragon, a recurring theme in Gaudí's work, referencing Saint George.

Ascending an oval staircase surrounding the colorful dragon, I reached a veritable forest comprising dozens of columns with tiled mosaics. A tour guide explained to a nearby group of sun-burned Brits that the Sala Hipòstila was supposed to be a market-place, saving its patrons from long treks to the city. On this day, however, it served as a colonnaded music hall.

A dark-haired flamenco guitarist informally turned out in a matching black oxford shirt and black pants began gently plucking away in the beautiful venue, creating haunting echoes. Minutes into the piece, the guitarist's partner, sitting on a soapbox-like instrument, began tapping its side, producing a rhythmic, per-cussive syncopation that reverberated through the Sala.

The two musicians reached a crescendo, at which point the percussionist stood up and struck a dramatic pose, his arms out-stretched, knees slightly bent, and face exuding studied wari-ness. For a moment he remained still. Then his wrists began to twist in curlicue-like flourishes as he slowly rotated. As the music swelled, he dramatically stomped his left foot, followed by his right. With the onlookers clapping, the dancing percussionist picked up speed, his arms gracefully aloft and his foot stomps increasingly pronounced and rapid until they tapped out a mes-merizing staccato beat. Every so often, he also clapped and swiftly rotated like a whirling dervish, never losing rhythm, while his hands periodically twirled above his head.

"*Olé!*" a woman to my left shouted, followed by another

and then another by other onlookers. The guitarist, for his part, strummed with increasing vigor, his hands in blurred motion and his face a tight grimace, as if excavating notes from his instrument was arduous.

With a series of macho poses—chest puffed out, hands aloft, body askew—punctuating the hypnotic spins and rapid, tap-like bursts, the impromptu performance came to a rousing end, prompting rapturous applause. The dancer, whose face dripped with sweat, bowed graciously and sat back down on his instrument.

Struck by his naked display of emotion, I dropped several euros in the performers' open guitar case and followed a colonnaded footpath with curved vaulting and leaning columns made from stones and capped by plants. A vague citrus scent permeated the air. In the high reaches of nearby trees, monk parrots, named for the hood-like ornamentation on their crowns and bright green and gray plumage, cackled rowdily at each other. The path took me past several gingerbread-like houses with mosaic roofs and exotic cacti that grew in all shapes and sizes. It was a fairyland.

Meandering my way through the Parc, I happened on its terrace overlooking the city atop the Sala Hipòstila. I sat down on a curving, mosaic bench, taking in a sweeping view of Barcelona. Set in a bowl, the city was bookended by two landmarks. Behind the city to the northwest was Tibidabo, a mountaintop whose name came from the Latin phrase "I will give you"—the words spoken by the Devil to Jesus when tempting him with the world's kingdoms. To my right was Montjuïc, or "Jew Mountain" in medieval Catalan, so named as it had once housed an ancient Jewish cemetery and, later, fortifications.

From my vantage point, I could take in the city's most conspicuous features, the spires of Sagrada Familia, Gaudí's still-unfinished

Roman Catholic basilica. On this cloudless day, though, I was most struck by the ocean, which was sparkling incandescently in the morning sun. Spaniards, beneficently positioned on the coastline of such a pristine body of water, had naturally become great seafarers. Conquering faraway lands in the New World, it seemed, was practically preordained. I gazed at the glorious expanse for fifteen minutes. The view was spellbinding, though the serenity of the moment was interrupted by a sudden onset of anxiety that departed as quickly as it had manifested. Perturbed by the unexpected disturbance, I retreated, once again passing the mosaic, salamander-like creature at the park's entrance.

After a short ride aboard the tourist bus, I alighted at Sagrada Familia, whose construction, well over hundred years on, remained incomplete, though its many finished portions were accessible to visitors. The church's richly decorated exterior with stone-carved biblical images and towers—some representing Christ, the Virgin Mary, four evangelists, and twelve apostles—was complete and decorated with whimsical mosaics. But the basilica's interior was even more remarkable. Its central nave vaulting was a forest of sloping, ribbed columns that rose upward, sprouting like plants as they neared a catacomb-like ceiling so stunningly ornate as to induce an ethereal sensation that overwhelmed and awed. So overpowering was the sensation that I averted my gaze momentarily. The sight had to be processed piecemeal.

Afterward, still gloriously struck by the basilica, I ducked into a small bakery across the street and bought a sandwich before again boarding the bus. I got off at another of Gaudí's masterpieces, the Casa Batlló, a colorful building whose facade, combining sculpted stonework and irregularly shaped windows, was decorated with mosaics constructed of broken ceramic tiles.

Seemingly, no linear lines graced the structure, which evoked some dragon-like beast, perhaps another allusion to Saint George.

From there, it was short walk to Plaza Catalunya and down the Rambla toward the Barri Gòtic. Although it was only midafternoon, I was tired and decided to turn in early. Lying on the couch back at the apartment, I wondered whether I was, as Gita claimed, a coward fleeing my troubles. Was I being impulsive and irresponsible? Was this whole plan of mine not a plan at all but an elaborate ruse to avoid adult obligations? I began to fade, overwhelmed by jet lag. I fell asleep without resolution.

RESIGNATION

Over the following days, I continued my pleasant journeys around the city, hitting the scenic overlooks at Tibidabo and Montjuïc, the beach and various museums, markets, and neighborhoods. Aside from a token conversation here and there with a waiter or shop owner, I barely interacted with anyone. It struck me one day that I had barely uttered a word. But I was not lonely. On the contrary, freedom from the falsity of contrived conversations, especially forced workplace chitchat, was liberating. Quietude permitted the internal voices stifled by everyday life to become more prominent.

Yet one of the internal voices kept raising concern about my decision to relocate to Spain. In such moments, I felt panicked and distraught. It was alarming. As a result, I began to ponder ways to reverse course. I could not, obviously, return to Marshall Cooper, tail between my legs, and plead for my job back. That would be crawling back into the lion's den, but I could find a comparable job in New York. I could be back in a familiar routine in weeks. I could reboot my reboot. I began brainstorming how I could approach Anna to rescind my six-month lease with her sister and brother-in-law while at once reaching out to headhunters in New York. It was doable. The loose ends could be tied up within days, and I could be home in a week. Ten days max.

One evening, I tapped out an email to a headhunter that Alex had put me in touch with earlier, when I was contemplating leaving Marshall Cooper. I wrote that I was again in search of employment, only more urgently. I needed something—quick! The headhunter replied overnight. My inquiry, he explained, was ill-timed, as the still-fragile job market was flush with recent college and business school grads as well as experienced hands still seeking regular employment after being fired during the crisis. "I'll shop your resume around," he wrote, "but I think it'll take time 'til it gets any nibbles." I tried another headhunter and received the same feedback. The job market, the second confirmed, was saturated. It would take a while to find a position.

Returning to New York to reclaim an approximation of my former life was not in the immediate cards. Some hiatus would be necessary. I took the setback in stride and began assessing how to bide my time. I decided to investigate the language school mentioned by Józef. Located in an inconspicuous building on a side street not far from Plaça de Catalunya, Vive had five small classrooms, a single front office, and a language library. It shared a floor with an Asian food store, some of whose clientele, it seemed, might benefit from its services.

José, the school's director, a short, stocky, jovial man with glasses so thick they might have deflected heavy ammunition, welcomed me into his office. After kindly tolerating my embarrassing accent for a few minutes, he administered an exam gauging my language proficiency. I scored on the low end of the intermediate scale.

Vive offered an array of inexpensive, one-month courses. I signed up for daily three-hour morning sessions. Any more than that, I figured, would wear me out. The courses began the following week. There were five other students: three from Hungary and one each from the Czech Republic and Greece. All were in their early- to mid-twenties and had come to Spain in search of work, which seemed odd given the country's economic doldrums.

Marco, our instructor, who looked roughly my age, was medium height and stocky. He had kind brown eyes, a pudgy nose, and a neatly trimmed beard. He strode into class on the first day casually attired in jeans, an oxford shirt, and sandals. "Hola, señores y señoras," he said, beaming. In Spanish, he introduced himself, explaining he was from a small town near Malaga in southern Spain and that he had been teaching for three years after a short-lived career in archeology.

He asked us to introduce ourselves in Spanish, which each of us did with varying success, before he explained the class's format, a combination of grammar lessons coupled with conversation exercises and the occasional video or film. The rest of the morning was spent on an intense review of verb tenses, a cauldron of confusing conjugations with as many exceptions as rules. It was exhausting. Yet Marco's good humor kept the lesson engaging and I left happy with my decision to enroll.

My initial impression was accurate. Though the classes were difficult and taxing—a sort of mental calisthenics as exhausting as the physical variety—I enjoyed them immensely. And I was a quick study. I also liked my classmates, who were good humored and friendly. The daily regimen also suited me, adding some necessary structure to my day. In addition, the panic attacks began to subside.

"I'm so glad to hear that you're doing well," my mother said weeks into my arrival. "I was so worried about you. Leaving your job and moving to Spain was so abrupt. What was I to think? But you seem to have landed on your feet. And I'm sure that you'll easily relearn the Spanish you acquired in school, especially now that you're going to language class. You know, I didn't speak a lick of French before your father and I went to Africa in the Peace Corps. It was difficult. Full immersion. Sink or swim. But I survived, and so will you."

I thanked my mother for the encouragement. "I'll be fine, Mom."

"Yes, you will. Change is always hard. Your father and I know that well. We've made a life of change, one after the next. It never gets easier, but I wouldn't have it any other way. Take the latest change. Moving to California hasn't been a cakewalk. Sure, the weather is fantastic. And we're near Los Angeles and San Diego and many other fascinating places. But life never works out the way you anticipate. Our first few months out here have been hard. Your father, for one, finds his students rather disengaged. They're just not that serious about learning. Maybe they'll get more serious as the term goes on. Or perhaps it just a generational thing. He's rather disappointed. Me, I am still adjusting. Like I said, I love the dry desert climate. It's such a refreshing change. And the geography around here is spectacular. It's parched inland, but you don't have to go far for rolling hills. The ocean isn't far away either. Neither is Mexico…"

My mother's methodical recounting allowed me to drift off in thought. It was likely I would have to kill at least another month in Barcelona, since an immediate about-face was impossible, at least if I intended to return to New York with a job. That was fine, since my Spanish course at Vive was a pleasant diversion, but I still had ample time of my hands, leaving me at loose ends in the afternoons.

I needed more.

An unexpected opportunity arose the following week. During class, Marco invited the group out to celebrate completing a particularly difficult lesson on the subjunctive tense. We congregated after class at a small bar around the corner and, over beers and finger food, got into conversation in twos and threes.

It was the first time I had spoken to any of my classmates in depth and, by dint of the seating arrangement, got talking to Althaia. A short, round-faced twenty-something from Athens, Althaia had lost her job at an accounting firm and, seeking adventure and new employment, had flown to Spain. She liked Barcelona but missed her family and was considering returning home.

Our back-and-forth was conducted in Spanish and English and, like an uncooperative lawnmower with stunted blades, required multiple retreads to complete the task. Athaia's impression of Spain as well-ordered and efficient, if slightly staid, ran counter to my own, reflecting our differing frames of reference. "We Greeks haven't had things together since ancient times," she observed sardonically.

As the afternoon wore on, most of my classmates departed, whittling down our numbers. At this point I began chatting with Marco, who related that he enjoyed his job, but his passion was archeology. He'd studied the discipline in school and later gone on a dig in Jordan. Unfortunately, the work was intermittent, so he'd sought other opportunities, trying social work before going into teaching.

Having struggled to find job security, Marco was struck by my own decision to jump into the employment abyss, which I recounted in my unsteady Spanish, mangling the verb tenses we had just gone over earlier in the day.

"Our journeys were quite different," he observed before sipping his beer. "I left a field I loved because it didn't pay, and you voluntarily gave up a well-paying job that you hated. Yet here we are. How long are you planning on staying in Spain?"

"I'm not sure," I replied. "I thought six months at first. Then I decided to return to New York right away. Now, I have no idea."

"That's brave of you. Job security was too important for me to stick with archeology. Perhaps I was cowardly, as I know that I'll never find any other job that I'll love as much. But I grew up without money, so I have good reason to be the way I am. I can't live hand-to-mouth. That's not for anyone, and certainly not me."

"I understand," I said. "I had the luxury to make a dumb decision. I had savings. But even if I stay for the time being, ultimately I'll probably end up back in the same sort of job that I left after my money runs out. You can't escape reality forever."

"No, you can't," Marco agreed. "So, if you don't mind my asking, how much money do you have? I mean, not the actual amount, but enough for how long?"

"I'm not sure. Seven or eight months maybe. Why?"

"Well, my brother-in-law owns a restaurant on the other side of town. It's nothing fancy—just typical Spanish food. It's got a nice bar, though. The place is really busy during football matches. He's always looking for kitchen help, mostly dishwashers.

"It's not glamorous work—I know, as I occasionally help out in a pinch. The kitchen is an inferno. But it can be fun. Anyway, Jordi, my brother-in-law, has trouble finding reliable people.

Mostly, he hires Guatemalans or Hondurans, who are wonderful, but they tend to leave once they've found something better.

"If you want to earn a bit of money, I'm sure he'd be happy to take you on. Like I said, it's tough work, but perhaps it would be a way of making some pocket change."

I thanked Marco for his generous offer, but explained that I was in Spain on a tourist visa and had no right to work.

"Don't worry, you'd get paid under the table. This is Spain!"

Trading white- for blue-collar work in a blazing hot kitchen constituted a remarkable feat of downward mobility. It was the sort of dizzying fall typically associated with high-flying Wall Street bankers caught in rotten schemes and ordered by a judge to do some lowly community service work as part of their sentence. No such riches-to-rags feats occurred voluntarily. But mine had. What I did now, aside from reclaiming a responsible life in New York, an option unobtainable for the time being, was irrelevant. So why not take the plunge?

I informed Marco of my interest in his offer the following week, and a few days later he promised to introduce me to his brother-in-law. He made good on his offer a week later by inviting me across town to a gritty, working-class neighborhood unlikely to be featured on any tourist brochure. Laundry hung from apartment terraces, and blaring sirens reverberated down the narrow streets.

As we turned a corner, two young girls in their early teens approached. Both had dark hair and eyes, as well as matching olive complexions. They wore long dresses with woolen shawls. One was clutching a sleeping baby wrapped in blankets. With plaintive expressions, both gestured at the infant, and then uttered words I could not decipher.

The two homed in on me, apparently sensing from my bearing that I was a foreigner and therefore more susceptible to the power of persuasion. "Please," one asked in English, gesturing to the infant. "Please help. Please."

I declined politely. The two surrounded me, grasping hold of my arms. "Please. Please. Hungry."

I shook my head and shrugged. Their sorrowful eyes and pitiful gestures toward the sleeping child would have worn down my defenses, but Marco, his face twisted in reproach, spat what I presumed were curses and shushed the two away.

"*Gitanos*," he muttered disdainfully as the girls walked away. "Gypsies. They're everywhere in this neighborhood. Just ignore them."

I was taken aback by Marco's dismissive reaction, which seemed to bely the open-mindedness he projected in the classroom. Yet I raised no objection. Instead, I smiled at the Gypsies and moved on.

El Castell de Vidre, Jordi's restaurant, was situated on a charmless, dusty block with a pharmacy and several vacant storefronts. Under its red awning were several tables, one of which featured two old men playing a game of chess. Marco exchanged salutations to both in Catalan, then ushered me into the establishment.

The modest restaurant had about ten wooden tables adored with white-pressed linen, red candleholders, and utensils that sandwiched folded napkins into fans. The far wall was stone and had a small ledge on which was perched a cured leg of pig. The dining room's minimalist decorations included several reproductions of Spanish landscapes and the red-and-blue flag of Barça, the city's venerable soccer team. A large television hung above a bar on the far end of the establishment.

"*Hola*, Marco," said a smartly attired woman in a white blouse and black skirt, approaching the restaurant's foyer. "It's so nice to see you." She gave him a kiss on both cheeks.

"Belen, this is my American student, Liv. I think Jordi told you about him. He's interested in working here."

"Oh, that's right," Belen responded in unsteady English. "It is nice to meet you." She kissed me as she had Marco. "I'll tell Jordi you're here."

Belen disappeared in the back, at which point Marco gave me an impromptu tour of the small, empty restaurant. Minutes later, a tall man with a round face, small eyes and nose, and pair of large ears that protruded from each side of his receding hairline, emerged from the kitchen. Possessing a beefy neck and a beach-ball-like midsection, he had wiry, pogo-stick-like legs connected to a pair of similarly oversized feet. He walked duck-footed. The curious ensemble of physical features suggested that his Creator, perhaps running late, had carelessly mixed and matched available odds and ends, yielding a strange if instantly endearing outcome.

"*Hombre*," Jordi boomed in a low baritone before embracing Marco. They exchanged pleasantries before Marco introduced me.

"This is Liv," Marco said, patting me on the back.

"Ah, yes, the American," Jordi observed in Spanish. "You know, I don't like Americans. You supported Franco. But I'll make an exception in your case."

I was unsure how to respond, so I just nodded awkwardly.

"Don't mind him," Marco chimed in sarcastically. "He's a Catalan. They're all like that. You know the definition of a Catalan, don't you? Someone who loves *his* people but hates all others."

"Oh," Jordi bridled in protest. "That's not true. We Catalans love everyone. Except Madrileños," he added, referencing inhabitants of Madrid. "We don't like them, that's true. As long as you're not from Madrid, Liv, you're welcome here. And even if you were, you'd be welcome, provided you're not a Real fan," he chided, referencing Real Madrid, Barça's bitter rival.

Jordi gestured to a nearby table and encouraged us to take a seat. He ordered a round of beers and promptly began recounting his frustrations with an unreliable alcohol distributor. After a ten-minute rant, he took a gulp of his beer and turned to me. "So, Liv, Marco tells me that you might be interested in working here. Why does a rich American want to do manual labor?"

It was a good question. I explained I had more time than money and thus was looking for a means of earning something on the side. The explanation had the virtue of being true, at least partially, as well as being easy to convey in Spanish. Jordi was skeptical. "Really? What were you doing before you came to Spain?"

My reply fed Jordi's disbelief. "You left a good job in New York? Strange. But I've heard of stranger things. Listen here, I had a classmate who came from a good family. His father ran a successful business, and his mother was a nurse. He was a good student too. Very smart. He was going places. But about the time he won a scholarship to study in Geneva, he got interested in bullfighting. Bizarre. Bullfighting isn't popular in Catalonia. In fact, it's banned here. Besides, bullfighters tend to come from working-class backgrounds. But his mind was made up. He turned down the scholarship for bullfighter training in Seville. Crazy. But get this, he loved bullfighting—until he faced a full-sized bull for the first time. A few weeks later, he was back in school. Today he's a doctor. So maybe you're having a bullfighter moment, Liv. I hope you don't run away the second you getting into my 'bullring,'" he chuckled and patted me on the back, "but I'll be happy as long as you stick around a little while. Let me show you around."

Jordi ushered me to the back of the restaurant and through two swinging doors. A metal counter with heating lamps, on which plates of dishes would be placed by several cooks when the place was humming, was situated just beyond the door. Behind it was a bay of stovetops and ovens. A walk-in refrigerator stood against a back wall, and to its right was the dishwashing station. The latter had a long rack on which plastic pallets of dishes were placed.

Jordi walked me through the drill, spraying chunks of food off dishes left over from the night before with an overhead hose before pushing the pallet in which they resided into a steel dishwashing unit. By pulling a lever, the sides of the boxlike dishwasher enveloped the pallet and, when locked into position, began the two-minute cleaning cycle. When completed, Jordi cranked the lever in the opposite direction and removed the steaming pallet of clean dishes.

"That's all there is to it," he said.

After pointing out where the clean dishes went as well as other various points, Jordi introduced me to the evening crew: a head chef, two sous chefs, and a dishwasher. Three of the four were from Guatemala, and the fourth, the head chef, was Sicilian. "We're the United Nations here," Jordi joked.

After we rejoined Marco in the dining room, Jordi asked if I remained interested in the job and, if so, whether I could give him at least a four-month commitment. "I'll pay you under the table," he added, "which is how things work here in Spain. The formal economy is the informal one."

I agreed.

"Bravo," he said, slapping me on the shoulder. "My United Nations just grew larger." A handshake solidified the deal, confirming my remarkable descent in status. It was like Superman transforming into his Clark Kent alter ego, if Clark Kent were a day laborer, not a hotshot reporter at the Daily Planet.

The following week, I began work. Belen greeted me kindly when I arrived at the restaurant and shepherded me into my new lair in the kitchen, where I reintroduced myself to the same evening crew I'd met days earlier. All seemed skeptical of me, perhaps wondering whether I had some ulterior motive for the grubby work. "Okay, Yanqui," Carlo, the head chef, remarked, "Let's see what you've got."

He tossed me an apron and gave me another primer on the kitchen's layout, pointing out where clean pots and pans, dishes, and utensils were kept, and where garbage bags were placed on the back patio. He suggested I begin with several plastic pallets of dirty dishes next to the dishwasher. "In about an hour, we'll have a staff dinner. After that, once guests arrive, things will get busy. You won't be needing that," he added, pointing to my sweatshirt. "It gets hot in here."

I doused the first pallet with the hose, scouring some rice hardened on a serving spoon with a wire brush before pushing it into the dishwasher and pulling the lever, as Jordi had instructed. I repeated this twice more with two other pallets teeming with plates, bowls, and utensils before retrieving the still-hot dishes and silverware and returning them to their respective places in the kitchen.

Carlo, checking on me, gestured to a nearby sink, inside of which were piled five or six pots. "Those are from last night," he said. "They need cleaning, too. They're too big to put into the dishwasher, so you're going to have to do them by hand."

With the same wire brush I used earlier, I scraped the pans, which were caked with grime. Each took much effort to clean. By the time I had finished, one of the two sous chefs, Javier and Andres, would add to the pile. "Vamos, Yanqui," one might say, chiding me gently to hurry up. I surmised it was a sort of hazing to determine whether I had what it took.

I was determinedly scraping off a layer of encrusted egg on a pot when Javier approached and told me it was dinnertime. "Even dishwashers get time off to eat," he joked.

Around a table in the back of the empty restaurant, the kitchen staff, myself included, sat down to eat. The delicious meal, though leftovers, included a potato tortilla—a sort of omelet with onions and potatoes—Russian salad, and French bread lathered with tomato and olive oil. The others drank red wine, but I stuck with water.

"So, Yanqui, what brings you to Spain?" Javier asked.

The question spoke to the general skepticism of my motives. The kitchen staff, the restaurant's resident proletariat, seemed particularly flummoxed, none more than Javier.

An indigenous American, Javier had a dignified face whose sharp contours and deep rivets were presumably etched by life's rigors. Two small, untrusting eyes that seemed to constantly probe back and forth, as if on guard duty, framed a thin nose that sloped sharply toward his thick lips. His skin was the color of almond butter and, with the exception of his lined face, was smooth. Stoutly built, he reminded me of one of the figures splashed across Strickland's canvases.

I felt particularly self-conscious around him, as if he were sizing me up to discern on which side of the class divide I stood.

"Yes, Yanqui," echoed Andres, who had a roundish, less austere face than his countryman and seemed to be the restaurant's jester, always cracking jokes. "What are you doing here? Shouldn't you be, you know, plotting world domination?" He laughed merrily.

I played along.

"I am. My job here is only a disguise. I'm with the CIA."

The assertion, though clearly in jest, gave them a start. The three stopped eating and gazed at me quizzically.

"Yes, it's true. I'm here to overthrow the government. Nobody will know in my dishwasher disguise."

My audience was rapt.

"I'm going to need some help. Are you with me?"

All were silent. Finally, Carlo unleashed a wheezy smoker's laugh. "Okay, Yanqui, we're all on board. But we have to get through this shift beforehand. First fillets of pork and paella, then revolution!" He raised his wine glass, still laughing. "Let's drink to that."

Javier and Andres tentatively held up their glasses, apparently still not persuaded of my actual intentions. The jury was still out.

The staff meal proved a brief intermission before the evening rush. A soccer match drew a large crowd to the restaurant, unleashing chaos in the kitchen. I could barely clean and shelve one pallet of dishes before another was placed in the queue. So it went for hours. By midnight, when I returned home, I was so exhausted that I had trouble marshaling the energy to take off my filthy, sweat-soaked clothing to bathe.

Still, I felt gratified. My body was tired, yet my mind was energized. I had won. Seldom did victory smell this bad.

CHAPTER 10

HOPE

Routine is the signpost of a dull life but salvation for an insecure one. It was the latter for me. My newfound regimen—mostly Spanish class and work—brought a measure of stability to my ill-defined foreign excursion, which otherwise easily could have collapsed in a fit of depressive unwinding.

Regimentation offered other benefits. My Spanish improved dramatically, if unevenly. Language acquisition is a patchy process. Some days my synapses fired with precision and I could effortlessly converse. Other days, I was a bumbling wreck unable to articulate the most basic thought.

Meanwhile, work at the restaurant became pleasantly predictable. Having earned Carlo's confidence, I would occasionally slice vegetables, prepare sauces, and perform other tasks ahead of the evening rush, in addition to washing dishes. Andres similarly welcomed me into the kitchen fraternity, nominating me as his focus group of one for off-color jokes that, once tested, were circulated to a larger audience. Javier, perhaps not entirely sure whether I was in fact involved in clandestine skullduggery, was more reticent.

As a kitchen curio of unknown origin, I would probably always be treated cautiously.

Belen was a different story altogether. Tall and thin with a mane of thick strawberry-red hair, perhaps owing to a Celtic lineage, Belen belied the stereotype of Spanish women being raven-haired seductresses. Her delicate features—thin lips, often painted red, button nose, and small brown eyes—matched her retiring demeanor, as she spoke softly and rarely was frazzled, even during busy evenings.

Roughly my age, Belen, a trained archivist, worked part-time at the restaurant, arriving in the late afternoon from her other job in retail. She had been moonlighting as a maître d' since her schoolteacher husband was diagnosed with a rare kidney disease that required he quit his job to undergo treatment.

I took an instant liking to Belen. She was cheerful and warm and, as it happened, keen on improving her English. We often huddled together during the employee meal, she speaking English and me Spanish. It was our language exchange.

A few weeks into my tenure at the restaurant, Belen invited me to a party hosted by a childhood friend of her husband. It would be, she observed in pidgin English, an "occasion to discover friends"—an opportunity I could not refuse, given my nonexistent social circle.

Oscar lived in a prosaic apartment block in a working-class neighborhood. The residential area was charmless and drab, devoid of the delightful boutiques and cafés typically found in the city. Diesel exhaust from a busy nearby road caked the surrounding buildings' lower floors in ashen soot, like the carbonized remains of an inferno. Perhaps sensing my surprise at the area's unattractiveness when we got out of the taxi, Belen remarked, "Welcome to the other Barcelona. It's not all a fairy tale."

The two of us entered one of the nondescript apartment buildings and took an elevator to the ninth floor. Belen knocked on a door, from which the murmurings of voices and clinking of glasses was emanating. Raul, Belen's husband, who was anticipating our arrival, opened the door and embraced his wife. But for a pallid countenance, Raul looked the model of good health. Lanky and tall, he had thick black hair, a pronounced nose, two dark eyes set widely apart, and a protruding Adam's apple that rhythmically moved up and down when he spoke.

"It's a pleasure to meet you finally," he said in Spanish, pivoting in my direction. "Belen has spoken highly of you. Please, do come in."

Oscar's spacious apartment featured a large living room with several couches and a dining table, on which an assortment of hors d'oeuvres and bottles of wine were on display. The walls were decorated with several posters, including one of the Beatles, and in the far corner, atop a pedestal, was a tasteful sculpture of a ballerina. About two dozen people were busily immersed in conversation.

Belen, spotting an acquaintance, made a beeline across the room, leaving me alone with Raul, who offered me a drink. "What brought you to Spain?" he asked while pouring wine into a plastic cup.

My response, a baroque flood stream of non-sequiturs, cried out for help. "Sorry," I said, "I'm struggling today."

Raul took my incoherence in stride, noting that my Spanish was far better than his English. He related a humorous anecdote about a misbegotten attempt to order food at a diner in New York.

I was responding in kind with a story of my own when Belen marched over and, pulling me by the arm, corralled me to the far end of the living room. "I have someone I want you to meet."

We navigated our way through a tangle of partygoers before Belen deposited me in front of a stout woman whose back was to me. "Valeria," Belen said, tapping her friend on the shoulder. "This is my friend Liv, the American."

Valeria wheeled around and kissed me on both cheeks. "It's nice to meet you," she said.

"It's nice to meet you, too," I answered.

Valeria, Belen explained, taught English at the same school where Raul worked before his health issues intruded. I proceeded to ask Valeria, who had a roundish, disarming face that exuded tenderness, about where she had learned English, which precipitated a discussion about the language's complexity.

Unable to express a point in Spanish, I reverted to English, prompting Valeria to do the same. We carried on for some time, pleasantly exchanging observations.

"So you're American?" a voice interposed just behind me. I turned to face a tall man with neatly parted blond hair, a square jaw, and patrician nose. Two small brown eyes peered out behind a pair of rimless spectacles, giving him a certain menacing sophistication. While his Germanic looks vaguely resembled Alex's, he had none of my friend's disarming nonchalance. Rather, his proud manner projected condescension and snobbery.

Staring down at me from on high, he repeated in English, "You're American?" He then took a sip of the beer he was holding.

"I am. You?"

"I'm from Austria. It's a small country. Have you heard of it? Americans, you know..."

Agitated, I responded, "Of course. It's got lots of kangaroos, right?"

My snarky reply failed to generate a rise. "Why do so many Americans like Edward Schmidt?" Not waiting for a response, he continued, "He's got no experience. Relevant experience, that is. He's a radio host. Nothing more. What credentials are those to lead the country? And he's a racist. Americans think they're exceptional, that they're the best. But how can this be if they elect people like him?"

He had a point. But I was not disposed to concede any ground—not to this self-important snoop. Regardless, I got uneasy when foreigners criticized America. Perhaps it was tribal—carping was only permitted by insiders. Yet there was more to it. The U.S. was a conspicuous target, sometimes rightly, sometimes not. That was the price of power.

Being in the crosshairs becomes tedious and, having spent ample time fending off pointed questions about the U.S. to foreigner friends and acquaintances in the past, I was not disposed to the pastime, especially when it involved a smug European from a country whose own historical reckoning about its recent misdeeds hardly set a high bar.

"Well, I guess we're idiots," I replied ironically, not wanting to discuss the matter further, especially with someone far bigger than me who might well be drunk. "That's all there is to it."

"No, really, why are Americans supporting someone so unqualified?"

Valeria, sensing my growing irritation, graciously intervened, asserting she wanted to introduce me to a friend. She then tugged my arm in the direction of the kitchen and apologized when we were out of the Austrian's earshot. "I think he's the roommate of one of Oscar's colleagues. Before you arrived, he was pestering an Italian woman about her country's financial problems. What an ass! Oscar should be more careful about who he invites. Have you met him yet?"

"The ass?" I joked. "I think I just did."

Valarie pitched back, giggling. "No, I mean Oscar."

"Not yet. Which one is he?"

Valeria scanned the living room and discreetly pointed in the general direction of the patch of real estate in the living room we had just vacated. "There, that's him."

I only saw a scrum of partygoers.

"There," Valeria repeated.

Instead of spotting him, I spotted her. Dressed in jeans and a white blouse, she was standing in profile roughly fifteen feet away, glass in hand, engaged in conversation with a bearded man in a plaid shirt. She had flowing black hair that fell down her shoulders, sublime olive skin, gently sloping nose, and delicate lips. Of medium stature, she was thin though shapely.

"See him?" Valeria asked.

"Yes," I replied apocryphally, my attention fixed elsewhere.

"He's an internist," Valeria added. "I hear his patients love him. Everyone does. He's a gem."

Presuming that this irresistible charmer was, in fact, the same guy chatting up the gorgeous object of my attention, a pang of jealousy coursed through my body. "Oh," I replied insincerely, "I'd love to meet him."

"Hey," Belen burst in, "you're not going to believe this, but Lukas is here."

"Lukas?" Valeria asked.

"Yes, Lukas—you know, that roommate of Oscar's colleague. He's here!"

"Oh, that's his name," Valeria replied. "Unfortunately, we already ran into him. He wanted to know why so many Americans are supporting that presidential candidate with the weird hair. Can you imagine that? Poor Liv, he'd barely walked in the door when he crossed paths with that nut." Valeria shrieked with laughter.

Belen explained that Lukas was a conundrum. He was a crack lawyer who had won acclaim for his noble advocacy at a Catholic charity dedicated to protecting refugee rights. Oscar and others insisted he was charming and kind—when sober. Yet several drinks were enough to transform the human rights defender into a self-important troll. He would seek out his marks and pepper them with obnoxious questions. His reputation made him an unwelcome guest to any party where alcohol was served, but somehow he had managed to slip through the cracks this evening.

The strange anecdote sparked a conversation between the two about the differences between southern and northern Europeans. Belen was recounting a trip to Berlin when I turned subtly to spot the pretty woman. I scanned the rest of the living room to no avail.

She was nowhere to be found.

Deflated, I returned my attention back to Belen and Valeria, who were carrying on gaily. So engrossed were the two that they might have happily chatted for hours but for an invitation to take a smoke break from Raul, who suddenly reappeared. "Oh, absolutely," Valeria gasped, pulling from her purse a pack of cigarettes.

Raul, turning to me, asked if I smoked. I shook my head. "Do come outside with us anyway," Valeria pleaded. "It's so hot in here. Plus, if you stay in here, you might run into Lukas again!"

The four of us exited the apartment, took the elevator to the ground level, and crossed the busy road to a small paved square situated between traffic lanes. With cars whizzing by, it was not terribly peaceful, but the fresh air was invigorating.

It did not last.

Belen, Raul, and Valeria lit cigarettes simultaneously, creating a smoky murk, as if a small pile of autumn leaves had been kindled. I braved smoke inhalation for several minutes before politely excusing myself, claiming I wanted to get a closer look at a large sculpture at the far end of the plaza.

The sculpture featured two large bronzes, one atop a tall pedestal and the other situated at its base. The piece crowning the pedestal resembled a stylized male torso—headless and armless—angled subtly toward the ground. It seemed to have been originally coated in a golden patina but was now splotchy and smog-tainted. At its base was a rock-impaled helmet with tendrils of apparent muscle and cartilage emanating from its severed neck.

I stood gazing at the morbid work, attempting to tease out its meaning.

"That's David and Goliath," a female voice remarked in Spanish from behind me.

I turned to find the beautiful woman from Raul's apartment smiling at me. She was as striking up close as she was from afar. Her proximity revealed a pair of chestnut eyes that matched her hair. Her pronounced cheekbones sat high on her slightly round, cherubic face. She was thinner than she'd appeared earlier, and a touch taller. Superficially, she resembled Gita. Both were dark-haired and complected, both were roughly the same height, and both shared a similar physique. However, whereas Gita's fundamental self-centeredness was all-encompassing and indomitable, like a large planetary body whose gravity enveloped all celestial mass in its vicinity, this woman's body language—her gentle movements—exuded tenderness and warmth.

"It's there in honor of the International Brigades—the volunteers who came from around the world to fight Franco in the Spanish Civil War. See, there." She pointed to an inscription that had the artist's name along with a quotation lauding the foreigners who'd rallied in defense on the democratically-elected government against the fascist forces.

"In Spain's case, however, Goliath won. We Spaniards don't want to face that, which explains why the piece is here, in an out-of-the-way place. It's still too painful.

"I'm Esperanza, by the way."

"I'm Liv."

"Leev?" she asked, mispronouncing my name. She peered at me inquiringly with her exquisite chestnut eyes.

I struggled to focus. "Yes, Liv."

"What sort of name is that?"

"It's short for Livingstone," I responded.

"Oh. That's unusual. Where are you from?"

"The U.S."

"What are you doing here?" she asked, her puzzled expression unchanged.

"I work in a restaurant. That's why I'm here—at the party, I mean. I work with Belen. Do you know her?"

Esperanza shrugged.

"She's Raul's husband. Do you know Raul?"

Esperanza shrugged again.

Explaining the complicated connection would require drawing a chart. What did it matter anyway? "Well, Raul is friends with Oscar, who's hosting the party. That may be wrong. It's a bit confusing. So, how is it that you ended up at the party?"

"My roommate is a friend of a friend of some guy who knows Oscar." Esperanza laughed at her explanation. "I was out with my roommate when she ran into a friend who invited us to the party. So here I am."

"Why are you here, though?" I inquired, referencing the plaza.

"Here? It was so hot and crowded in the apartment. I needed some fresh air. I'm with them." Esperanza pointed to the other end of the plaza where a few silhouettes stood, cigarette smoke emanating from their shadowed forms.

"You don't smoke, either?"

"No. It's an awful habit. You do ask a lot of questions, Leev."

"You think so?" I responded impishly.

Esperanza giggled.

"So, Spaniards don't want to face their history?"

"There you go again. Are you sure you're not a journalist? Or spy? Do you really work in a restaurant?" She tilted her head to the side and squinted.

"I do ask too many questions," I shrugged, "Sorry."

"No need to apologize," she replied, reaching out and touching my arm reassuringly. I felt a jolt course through my body, followed by embarrassment for possibly telegraphing my elation. But there was no indication that she noticed. The pleasing gesture took me by surprise. Physical touch between strangers of the opposite sex is not common in the U.S. For the most part, that's probably a good thing. It avoids misapprehensions. Customs are different in Spain; no such prohibition exists.

"Spaniards don't want to face our history," Esperanza admitted. Switching to English, she added, "'The past is never dead. It's not even past.' Didn't an American writer say that?"

"I'm not sure. I'm impressed regardless. How do you know about American writers?"

"I've always liked literature. And I'm a journalist, so I do appreciate good writing."

"You're a journalist?" I asked.

"Yes, I cover politics for a small newspaper."

Presently, the bearded man in the plaid shirt with whom Esperanza had been talking when I'd first laid eyes on her at the party emerged from the shadows. Apparently, this was not Oscar the irresistible charmer, as I had assumed earlier. Not by a long shot. He looked me over as he approached, frowning disdainfully before turning his attention back to Esperanza.

"Do you want to go?" he asked sharply. "I do. We're expected at Lucia's anyway."

"Okay. By the way, this is Leev," she said, still mispronouncing my name. "He's American."

The bearded man, nodding wanly, said nothing. No, this definitely was not Oscar, but at least he did not go on some rant about Schmidt. For that I was grateful. Instead, he addressed Esperanza. "Let's go."

"Well," Esperanza remarked, "it was very nice meeting you."

"Likewise," I replied.

Esperanza turned and took a few steps away before pivoting back in my direction. "Oh, wait," she said, reaching into her purse and retrieving a business card. "If you want to know more about subscription fees, send me an email."

Confused, I took the card.

"Bye," she said with a wink before leaving.

I thanked her and turned toward the sculpture with studied nonchalance, but promptly craned my head to watch her depart. As she neared the far end of the plaza, I stood on my tiptoes to catch a final glimpse. Then she was gone.

CHAPTER 11

MAKING AMERICA GREAT AGAIN

ating etiquette is a drag. When searching for romance, one must do this and not that, and do it now and not then, or face the consequences. I did not need to play the game when I was with Gita. Being single changed that. Now I had to adhere to the unwritten rules or risk joining Strickland in bachelor purgatory.

As a result, I could not reach out to Esperanza the day after we met. That would be an amateur mistake of the highest order, likely indicating a lack of confidence in my market value or, worse, desperation. I had to play it cool. So, I waited at least a few days to contact her, facetiously inquiring into a newspaper subscription. While I was confident she'd reply, since she had slipped me her business card in the first place, I had no idea what her intentions were. All the same, I waited patiently for her to write back, which she did days later, informing me she would write more when she returned from a trip.

The same day, I received an inquiry from my New York–based

headhunter regarding two bank jobs. Neither seemed a good match, given my not having a background in finance, but the headhunter assured me otherwise. The employers, he said, were interested. To pursue both, I would have to return to New York for face-to-face interviews. This would not be difficult, as a speedy trip would necessitate my missing just a few days of work, about which I now felt a curious sense of responsibility. Thus, I bought some time by asking the headhunter to confirm specific dates for the interviews.

A few days later, after checking my in-box for a message from the headhunter, I scanned the headlines, many of which referenced a major speech given by Schmidt in Ames, Iowa, ahead of that state's all-important caucus formally kicking off the nominating contest. The theatrics had begun before the radio personality/presidential candidate's address at a convention hall decorated in red, white, and blue bunting. Several hundred of his supporters, many wearing hats featuring the Comitan's insignia—an eagle with a snake in its beak—packed the venue. Intermittently, they shouted insults at the press, who were cordoned off in a far corner of the hall, protected by several beefy security guards.

Schmidt's current wife, a one-time stripper from Ukraine in a form-fitting dress, warmed the crowd with a short speech. One article noted that it had been hard to hear over whistles and catcalls, but she seemed pleased by the raucous response. Schmidt then appeared on stage in a dark suit and yellow tie. His radiant orange hair, worn in a pompadour, glistened in the spotlight. He waved to his supports and, turning toward the press, grabbed his crotch, prompting the crowd to erupt in cheers.

Schmidt basked in the glow for several minutes, before hugging and kissing each of the dozen American flags arranged in a line at the back of the stage. Afterward, he embraced his wife and gave her a pat on her backside. Just then, a protester holding a sign that read "Hate Isn't American" stood up, but a man in a Comitan hat immediately punched him. Security guards, fearing for the protester's life, accompanied him out. Schmidt praised the pugnacious Comitan.

Speaking off a teleprompter, he ominously warned that America faced an existential crisis. "I need not remind you of that which you know. It is winter in America. Legions of evildoers hiding in plain sight, testament to their fearlessness, threaten to destroy us from within and without. You know who they are. They comprise, firstly, malefactors of great wealth, whose greed is as boundless as their patriotism is limited. These stateless parasites reside in the foul fortresses of finance, where nations' fates are at their casual whimsy. They buy and sell and sell and buy with no interest but their own. Greed is their currency, and currency is their creed."

Schmidt had singled out for condemnation several prominent businessmen and political leaders, all of whom were either dark-skinned or Jewish, and followed with a long-winded rant about immigration. He then segued into a dark tangent about rising crime before closing on a more optimistic note.

"Friends, I am here to restore prosperity to this great land. I am here to restore law and order. I am here to restore liberty. I am here to restore freedom. And I am here to restore God Almighty. America, my friends, will be great again! Some may criticize my ambition. Some may call it grandiose, unwise. It is neither. Rather, it is calibrated to address the great challenges before us. And from those great challenges we will not shrink. I, my friends, will not shrink.

"And so I promise you this and this alone: America will start winning again, winning like never before. America will come first. America, my friends, will be great again!

"Thank you, and may God bless this great nation."

The speech, interrupted frequently by chants of "U-S-A," was astounding. More astounding was what followed next. Later that evening, hundreds of Comitans gathered in a park near the convention hall. Wearing military fatigues and carrying TIKI™ torches, they had marched through town chanting, "Hispanics, Muslims, Blacks, and Jews, either way, we all lose." They had stopped mid-way to hear speeches, including from the owner of a chain of popular restaurants repeatedly fined for hiring illegal immigrants, before clashing with counterdemonstrators back at the park. One woman died.

Meanwhile, Comitan rallies continued apace. In one rally in Tuscaloosa, Alabama, fistfights erupted between the right-wing agitators and counterdemonstrators, injuring scores. In another rally in Eugene, Oregon, Comitans joined forces with a local militia to occupy a courthouse. They refused to leave until government representatives agreed to designate as sovereign territory a ranch owned by a local firebrand who owed millions in back taxes.

Days later, a Mississippi Comitan member, wearing a swastika on his arm, walked into a family-planning clinic in Jackson and opened fire with a shotgun while yelling, "Die, abortionists!" Six were murdered, including two pregnant women. Schmidt refused to condemn the violence. He even tacitly endorsed it. "I remind you of what Thomas Jefferson once said: 'The tree of liberty must be refreshed from time to time with the blood of patriots and tyrants.'"

His disqualifying behavior proved otherwise. Polls had him trouncing his rivals, as his acid tongue and wanton mendacity, defying logic, only aided his campaign. I could not believe what was happening. I did not recognize my country. The Comitans had begun to make their presence felt in New York before I left. One had even assaulted me. They had contributed to my overall unhappiness, culminating in my departure for Spain, but I never imagined the situation would get this bad. Schmidt seemed like a joke. He wasn't. His election appeared more likely by the day. How could I return to the U.S? It was becoming a wasteland of bigotry and hate.

Upset by the breathtaking series of events, I gave Alex a call. Like me, he was aghast, though not entirely surprised. His colleagues' reaction to Schmidt's rise indicated that tolerance for intolerance could be found in unexpected places. Most thought him a demagogue and buffoon, and cringed at his racism and xenophobia, but they also anticipated that, if elected, he would cut their taxes. For that, all sins were forgiven.

Alex also relayed his impressions of a recent camping trip in the Shenandoah Valley. After hiking for a few days, he visited a friend at his family's home in West Virginia. He found the area strikingly beautiful, but also depressing. One town after the next was gutted. Each had a few box stores, crumbling village center, and church or two. Nothing more.

"These places had functioning factories and mines at one time. They may have never been wealthy, but their residents managed to eke out a living, as they had for generations. That time has passed. Now they're meth-riddled ratholes. And it's not just a consequence of the financial crisis. The decline has been going on for decades."

His friend had pointed out that that the working class's falling status was reflected in the size of pickup trucks. It was an inverse relationship. Ten or twenty years ago, when the working class could still make a decent living, trucks were much smaller. Now they were huge. "They've got to feel empowered any way they can," his friend had observed. The story was not limited to Appalachia. A lot of the country was hurting. Alex noted that life expectancy for chunks of the working class was actually falling.

Had the Wall Street high-flyer suddenly grown a conscience? Was the plight of the workingman now a matter of great concern to him? I doubted it. More likely, it was just another example of how Alex seemed to have several distinct personas that somehow coexisted. Trying to reconcile them was foolhardy. Alex was and would always remain a mystery.

Regardless, I did not share his newfound sympathy for "Joe Sixpack." I had heard it all before. Countless apologists characterized the Comitans when they first appeared as economically troubled but otherwise decent people who formed the backbone of their communities. Circumstance was to blame, not them. I never bought it. Many others were hurting too, but they weren't acting like Brownshirts. Getting punched in the face by a scowling Comitan shouting an epithet removed any doubt. Intolerance wasn't a bug but a feature.

"Even if what you say is true," I replied, "why are the inhabitants of the places you visited in West Virginia and others like it turning to a conman? Schmidt's a charlatan. He has spent his career screwing people—working people, mostly—and he's going to do it again if elected."

"That's how it always works," Alex said. "Didn't you make that very point to me once? Turn natural allies against each other.

Divide and conquer. Like I said, lots of people are hurting. Badly. You just don't see it. Nor do most who move in our circles. The world has left them behind."

"So they're looking for a strongman to recreate a mythological past when life was good?"

"Exactly."

I was unmoved. "I'm not so sure. But it's ironic regardless. Conservatives supposedly are defined by skepticism of government. Bullshit. The Right objects to government only when government does things it doesn't like. When it controls government power, it's a different matter. Then watch out!

"The Right oftentimes has little patience for democracy. Democracy is cumbersome, messy. It involves compromise with political opponents, which implies recognizing the legitimacy of those with opposing views. Progress occurs in fits and starts.

"Many conservatives are authoritarians at heart and have no time for this. Which is why they spend so much time short-circuiting the democratic process—disenfranchising voters, gerrymandering districts, et cetera—and why they'll gladly support a crypto-fascist."

"You may be right," Alex responded, offering tepid endorsement. "But—"

"Of course you wouldn't agree with me," I shot back jokingly. "You're part of the elite! You and your colleagues—the ones you said grudgingly support the likes of Schmidt as long as they get their tax cuts. For fuck's sake. First you guys create the mess and then profit off it. It's heads I win, tails you lose. Quite the racket."

"Hey, tough guy, weren't you saying earlier that you're thinking of getting a job on Wall Street?"

I conceded the point.

"I agree with you—to some degree," Alex continued. "But I think you're missing the economic piece. Listen to this quote Strickland sent me. Hold on, let me find it." Alex tapped on his keyboard for a few moments. "Wait a second. Okay, here it is. It's from some academic or something. He's dead. Anyway, he wrote, 'The American Dream's demise kindles burning resentment among those deprived the opportunity to better themselves. As faith in conventional fixes through the legislative process wanes, it is replaced by anarchist-like rage, with the aim to utterly destroy the whole rotten system, and recreate from its ashes a mythological bygone era when society supposedly functioned as designed. Such is the forgotten man's revenge. The only question is who will be its vessel?'

"That's exactly what's happening. Those who've been screwed are looking for a 'vessel' who's going to 'make America great again.'"

"White-controlled, you mean," I corrected.

"Yeah, that too."

"That too? Racism isn't incidental. Blacks, Latinos, Jews— they're cast as the 'other.' A country controlled by whites is exactly what is meant by 'making America great again.' Too many people of color are acquiring what's the birthright of whites. It's fear of 'replacement.' We're experiencing a moral panic.

"Look at the Comitans. They don't even hide their hate. And why should this surprise? Race has always been the country's chief organizing principle.

"Voting patterns bear this out. Poor people who cite economic concerns as their chief preoccupation vote Left. They always have. In other words, class-consciousness is alive and well—for some. It's poor people, among others, who cite demographic changes as their chief preoccupation who vote Right and therefore against their economic interests. I wouldn't downplay the role that race plays."

"I get it," Alex responded. "But what I'm saying is that racism is primed by economic disenfranchisement. Scapegoats always crop up during bad times. That's how it always goes. But the real issue is the bad times—"

"And correctly identifying who's actually responsible for the bad times," I interjected.

"Exactly! Look, it was the guys a floor up from me at work whose reckless speculation in Latin America real estate made the ground beneath Buenos Aires slums more valuable on paper than Manhattan is, and they got away with it. When their casino gambling tanked the world economy, they escaped unscathed. No penalty. No jail. Nothing! Most got promotions, since the firm unloaded its shitty investments on unsuspecting clients before things went south. We made money! What the fuck? Even I was pissed, and I liked many of them, at least personally. But they should've been prosecuted. None were.

"That ticks people off. And you know what, they're right. What's more, the arrogant bastards a floor above me vote for Left-wing candidates. Not all—some just want tax breaks—but most have nothing in common with the 'unwashed masses.' They've got postgrad degrees and live in diverse cities. They're well traveled and well read. They support gay rights. They don't fall for the Right's bullshit. They're too savvy.

"Fortunately for them, so-called liberal politicians cater to their interests, not those of the working class. They support low corporate tax rates, free trade, and deregulation, and they're the champions of capital! So much for class consciousness. What good does it really do if there's nobody there to answer the call, since nobody truly represents the working class?"

"That's one way of looking at it," I responded. "The difference between the Left and Right may not be as great as it once was, but there's still a difference. And by voting for the Right, those in the working class are only screwing themselves.

"Regardless, there's never any defense for backing a bigot. I don't care how disenfranchised you are or think you are—or aren't at all. Racism is racism. It can't ever be justified."

"True," Alex responded. "But there's how things should be and how things are. They're different. People aren't rational. Take you, for example."

"Take me how?"

"Well," Alex replied sardonically, "you're having a pre-midlife crisis. There's no reason for it—"

"Yeah, there is," I protested. "I've always been precocious. You'll get there eventually. I'm just ahead of the curve."

"Seriously, how you doing?"

"I'm fine. Actually, better than fine. I like Barcelona. I've got a nice place and, well, a good job.

"Oh? Where?"

"At a restaurant. I'm a dishwasher."

"Your parents must be very proud."

"Very," I answered dryly. "I'm not sure if I'm sticking around, though." I then told him about my upcoming interviews. Alex was supportive, offering to put me up when I was in town. I then told him about Belen. It had been a long time since I felt such an immediate connection with someone, and this despite our language barrier. I also mentioned Esperanza. She, like Belen, seemed unusually kindhearted.

Alex was not surprised. He claimed American women, in their pursuit of equality, had shed those stereotypical feminine qualities—tenderness, cordiality, warmth—perceived to be totems of their servitude. To be treated on equal terms required becoming one of the guys. Foreign women, he added, tended to be different. They retained, even celebrated, their "female" dispositions instead of attempting to suppress them in an errant search for acceptance. "Apparently, you've been spending a lot of time with Strickland," I responded. "I can see why you're so close." He had laughed before getting off the phone, as it was early morning in New York, and he had to go to work.

When I hung up, I began to gather my belongings ahead of work. Oddly, as unnerving as the discussion of Schmidt's ascent had been, it was Alex's channeling of Strickland that had particularly rattled me. I could think of nothing but his unusual friend.

Strickland's decision to quit his lucrative job was inexplicable to me, even though I had done the same. Yet I did not see our actions as one; somehow, they differed in my mind, perhaps because his were irrevocable. He had left the business world for good, with no intention of returning. I had no confidence that I had the guts to do the same.

That evening at work, my brain was still consumed by Strickland. I wondered why he had not just kept his job and simply painted on the side, a more prudent course of action. I wondered whether he was making ends meet. But mostly I wondered how he'd negotiated the disdain that his decision evoked. How could he endure it?

When I returned home, I wrote to my headhunter, asking to postpone my interviews due to a scheduling conflict. I did not know what compelled me. I wanted to believe it was an act of

Strickland-like courage and that I, like him, could go against the grain. I had it in me. I could flout convention.

But that was a lie.

I did not have the courage of my convictions. I cared what others thought. I desperately sought affirmation. Indeed, it was precisely that the undeserving in my eyes, not me, often received affirmation that sparked my righteous indignation. Strickland would not care either way. But I did.

Still, I could not summon the will to return to New York to interview on Wall Street. It just did not seem right, so I backed out.

I sat in my apartment, alone in every sense of the word. Every breath I exhaled forged a deeper and more irreconcilable distance between my present and previous lives. There was a completeness, a fortitude, in my uncertainty.

CHAPTER 12

LA BOQUERIA

Esperanza suggested we meet at La Boqueria, the famous market located in my neighborhood, just off the Rambla. Her communication was terse, leaving instructions to rendezvous at a corner entrance. I was elated. I had spent the previous days in a state of such eager anticipation that it surprised even me. Initially, I had ascribed this to my relative isolation. I got on well with my colleagues at the restaurant and classmates from language class, but that still left quite a bit of time on my own. Perhaps, I wondered, my impatience was a function of loneliness. But I was wrong. Esperanza was special. This soon became clear. When I arrived, the market was a hive of activity, with thongs swarming the many kiosks selling coffee, delectable treats, and even parakeets trilling noisily in their cages.

As I was peering at my phone, I felt a tug on my sleeve. "Leev," Esperanza said boisterously, mispronouncing my name again. She kissed me on both cheeks and apologized. "I'm sorry for being late. I'm Spanish. It's in our genes."

Esperanza was luminous. Casually dressed in form-fitting jeans and a white sweater, with a plaid scarf playfully dangling from her neck and her handbag over her shoulder, she exuded a certain carefree charm that might have come off as arrogant were it not accompanied by a playful aura, as if she did not take herself too seriously. It was intoxicating.

I blushed.

"You haven't been here before? What a shame. La Boqueria is charming, and it's just around the corner from you! Very naughty," Esperanza noted impishly. "You Americans. I'll bet you've gone to a lot of fast-food restaurants since you've been here. Correct?"

"Of course," I replied emphatically. "We didn't become the world's fattest people without effort! It takes work. Hard work. But to be honest, I'm not terribly interested in the market." In butchered Spanish I added, "I only came today because of the newspaper subscription. I was hoping you could get me a discount."

"A discount?" Esperanza asked, eyebrows arched. "So that's why you're here?"

"That, and I thought you could introduce me to that charming guy with you in the plaza. I think we'd hit it off."

Esperanza laughed. "Sergio? If he finds out I'm here with you, he's not going to be so charming." Whether there was truth in her jest, I could not tell.

"Come," Esperanza said, grabbing my hand and leading me through the crowded market.

Housed in a voluminous modernist building with a metallic and stained-glass exterior, the temple of gastronomy featured a culinary cornucopia—meat to fruits to vegetables to candies and much more. It was sweeping and vast, colorful and pungent, and truly awe-inspiring.

"Well, this is going to be fun to see La Boqueria through your eyes," Esperanza remarked giddily, as she grabbed my hand and led me through the throng.

Eyes may be the windows to the soul, but hands tell a lot about a person, too. Esperanza's narrow fingers, capped with purple nail polish that resembled mini lollipops, were tender, delicate, and soft. Her grasp drew me in.

I was living a more honest life, free of meaningless office work and throwaway relationships, free of the false persona required by a phony existence. The thrill of Esperanza's touch stoked vulnerability, and vulnerability implied possible danger. I took note of it.

"This is my favorite part," Esperanza finally announced. "Right here."

Before us, tastefully laid out on ice, were scores of neatly aligned salt cod, about a foot in length. Next to them were several rows of salmon-colored fish with black eyes, about the same size, though more bulbous, and on the end a mound of sardines, which sparkled in the pale light. One stall over featured a glorious array of seafood: gelatinous octopus lumped together in congealed mounds, lobsters with their claws fastened with rubber bands, menacing crabs as big as dinner plates, silver-dollar-sized shellfish, and fire-engine red shrimp.

"I like fish, but it's not my favorite food," Esperanza observed. "Still, for some reason, I love this part of the market. It's nature's bounty. Do you know what seafood is called in Italian? *'Frutti di mare.'* Fruit of the ocean," she said in accented English. "It's perfect!"

"Yes, it is," I averred. "How can you be Spanish and not love seafood?"

"Well, I'll tell you a secret. I did love seafood, especially my mother's black paella made with squid ink. Delicious! And I still can't resist salmon. But a while back, I went to Greece with some friends. Three of my girlfriends and me joined their boyfriends and this guy I liked. It was going to be perfect. And everything was—at first. On the first night on this gorgeous island, we had dinner together on the patio of a restaurant overlooking the ocean. It was so romantic. The guy I was interested in was clearly interested in me." Esperanza's eyes then danced. "Love was in the air. The meal was an assortment of seafood served on an enormous oval, silver platter piled so high with fish, crabs, shrimp, and much more that two waiters had to serve it. We devoured the entire platter like famished inmates. Afterward, the table, which was covered in carcasses, looked as though it was the site of a *'masacre de mariscos'*—a seafood massacre. We decided to take a walk down to the water to stretch our legs. Then it hit. My friend Laia began complaining of stomach cramps. We laughed it off at first, blaming her ravenous appetite. But it quickly spread, like a virus. Within ten minutes, two of us had thrown up—right there on the beach! It was terrible!" Esperanza starting giggling, at first with restraint, then with unbridled mirth, prompting her to cover her mouth with her hand, using the other to grab hold of my arm for ballast. "I was so embarrassed. But what could I do? I had food poisoning. We all did!"

"That's awful!" I exclaimed.

"Yes, it was. For the next few days, all of us barely left our hotel rooms. We were all so sick. It ruined the whole vacation as well as my chances with the guy. For a few years, I could not even look at seafood without getting queasy. Even its smell was intolerable. Eventually, I developed a taste for it again, though not like before. To this day, I eat it only sparingly. Still, I like going to markets like this and seeing the many types of fish on display. I'm not sure why. Maybe it's because it's a reminder of the planet's richness."

"Except that the fish are dead," I playfully responded.

"Oh, Leev. Come this way," she urged, again grabbing hold of my hand.

We walked past stalls bursting with impossible arrays of fruit, nuts, dates, sweets, garlic, olives, and exotic vegetables that defied identification before nearing the portion of the market dedicated to meat. Pork and lamb chops and various cuts of meat were tastefully presented in display cases, above which chorizos of all types and sizes hung on racks next to massive pig legs, hooves affixed, the size of barbells—and probably as just as heavy.

"That's *jamón ibérico*," Esperanza clarified, pointing to the pigs' legs. "You know, cured ham. Have you ever had it?"

I winced, placing my hand over my mouth. "Oh no," I muttered.

"What is it?" Esperanza asked.

"This just reminds me…how do I say in Spanish? Disaster."

"Disaster?"

"When I first arrived, I went out with this beautiful woman. She was extraordinary. But over lunch, I ate some *jamón ibérico*. It must've been bad, because I threw up ten minutes later. Right there!"

Esperanza looked at me with confusion. Turning, I added, "Just looking at it makes me…I think I'm going to…" I burst out laughing.

"That's mean, Leev!" Esperanza protested, smiling broadly. "I thought you were serious."

"See, two of us can play that game."

Esperanza slapped me on the shoulder and took my hand

again. "Come," she urged. We meandered around the market for another half hour, with Esperanza playing tour guide, pointing out the derivation of particular foods, especially those from Spain. Afterward, we retreated to a corner bar and ordered two cups of tea to warm us up on the sunny but chilly day.

Noting her patriotic pride, I asked her where in Spain she was from. "I'm Madrileña," she said in a whisper. Sensing my confusion, she elaborated, "I'm from Madrid. But I can't say that too loud here, or I might get thrown out."

"So you're a Real Madrid fan?" I asked.

"Ostia, no!" she answered, using slang to denote surprise. "Never. Atlético Madrid is my team—the workingman's club," she elaborated with a laugh. "Well, not really. I never really cared for sports. I was a bad athlete myself. I once signed up to run 10 kilometers to raise money for some good cause, and it nearly killed me. Never did that again! But people's fascination with football—I don't get it. I mean, why be loyal to any club anyway? Its players are from around the world, and so are the owners. Besides, there's always another season, so the stakes are meaningless. Obviously, this is not a popular opinion. Football is a religion here."

I concurred, noting the many Barça flags that flew around the city. Esperanza rolled her eyes. The club once represented the region's national aspirations, she explained, while Real—'Royal' Madrid—was the avatar of unitary Spain, the monarchy and, of course, Franco himself. But all that had changed. The sport was just a product like any other. "It's a business," she observed. "Or worse, a diversion for the masses."

"Very Marxist of you," I parried.

Esperanza giggled. "Yeah, maybe. I came from a long line of

leftists. My great-grandfather went to jail during Franco's reign. He worked in a factory and was accused, rightly, of union organizing. It had a big impact of my grandfather, who recalled his own father's long absences during his incarceration. He shied away from politics himself, as does my father, who doesn't like to talk about current events, which is ironic, since my mother is a rabble-rouser. She grew up in a militant family in Seville; a few of her ancestors fought against the fascists. She always got into trouble with the authorities growing up. This worried her parents, of course."

"What do your parents do, Esperanza?"

"My father works in advertising, and my mother is a schoolteacher. They're very good people. I love them very much. What about you? What are you doing here, Leev?"

"I'm here to get a free newspaper subscription," I replied, straight-faced. "I thought that was clear."

"Silly! No, I mean what are you doing in Spain?"

"Well, I'll tell you that in a moment. But first let us finish with you. Why are you here in Barcelona if you're from Madrid?"

"I told you, Leev," Esperanza said in a whisper, "don't say that out loud. Do you want to get me arrested?"

I chuckled.

"Fine, if you want to know the truth, it was love. Esperanza's eyes started to dance again. "Love brought me to Barcelona. I met a guy in Madrid—an Italian studying architecture—and followed him here. It was that simple."

"You mean the guy in the plaza?"

Esperanza hesitated, and then, grasping the allusion, recoiled. "No, that's not Francesco."

Though confused, I decided not to pry. "Well, do you like it here?"

"Yes, I do, though it's not an easy place to feel at home if you're not local. The Catalans are insular. If you're not native Catalan, they keep you at arm's length. I've had a lot of trouble making friends. But the city has grown on me. I love how cosmopolitan and international it is. I don't like that it's overrun with tourists," she added, giving me a wink. "I mean, La Boqueria was a madhouse. It's the same in many parts of the city. You start to figure out which places to avoid, but it still gets tiring. I can see why the locals are so annoyed. I get it. Yet the setting is perfect. So yes, I do like it."

"And what about your work?" I probed.

Esperanza threw up her hands in despair. "Leev," she protested, "I feel like I'm being interrogated. Tell me about you!"

"I'm really boring, so if I tell you, I'll never see you again."

Esperanza smirked.

I proceeded. "What sorts of matters do you focus on at work?"

"Okay, if you must know, I am an environmental reporter. But we're a regional paper with a small circulation, so I have to do a bit of everything. I'm working on an investigative report about migrant laborers in the garment industry at the moment."

"Sounds fascinating."

"It is, but it has its downsides."

"And those are?"

"It doesn't pay much. I have another job to make ends meet. I help special-needs children, which is rewarding, but I do it for the money. Sorry, that sounds terrible..."

"No, it doesn't. It's just not your passion."

"Exactly, though it does have its moments. I work with one

teenager with severe dyslexia. We were doing a school project of hers together, and after I showed her some tricks to correctly identify some problem letters, she began to cry from joy. I couldn't help but cry too. That sort of thing never happens as a journalist. Still, I love the hunt. You know, pursuing bad guys. There's nothing like it. Okay, Mr. Mystery, now it's your turn. Why are you in Spain?"

I did not want to delve into the topic. My Spanish was not up to the task. Besides, the many reasons I uprooted my life were still being crystallized in my own mind. It was an ongoing process. How was I going to convey that without looking dumb? "I'm not really sure," I answered accurately. "I was working in a job that I didn't like…"

"At a restaurant?"

"No, I'm only working at a restaurant now to—well, I'm not sure why. Anyway, I was working in a corporate job in New York and—"

"What sort of corporate job?"

I hesitated, unable to conjure an explanation in a foreign tongue. "I researched politics and economics," I replied stiltedly. "It's hard to explain in Spanish. But I didn't like it."

"So you just quit?"

"Yes. I just quit."

"Was there more to it?"

"Probably."

"A girl?"

"Well, there was a girl, but she wasn't that important. I mean our relationship wasn't that important. It was terrible, in fact. And I didn't like my job, so I thought I'd just, well, leave."

"That's why you're here washing dishes?" Esperanza asked with confusion.

"Like I said, it's hard to explain in Spanish."

Esperanza, switching tacks, asked why I had come to Barcelona. I clarified that, for the most part, it was arbitrary. I wanted to work on my Spanish and had thought that the city's seaside location would be ideal. I attempted to turn the tables, asking Esperanza how she'd gotten into journalism, but she pushed back.

"You're doing it again. You're avoiding my questions."

"Okay," I said earnestly. "The truth is that I got in trouble at home."

"Really? What kind of trouble?"

"Well, I was caught…" I said, pausing dramatically, "breaking the law. Robbery."

Esperanza stared blankly at me in disbelief.

"Well, not really."

Esperanza rolled her eyes again. "You know, you're so enigmatic that I might've believed you."

Given our shared reticence, I proposed a compromise, suggesting Esperanza tell me more about Spain. Specifically, I asked again why Spaniards did not want to face their history. This broke the impasse, as Esperanza gladly elaborated, occasionally seasoning her insights with personal anecdotes.

Spain, she explained, was deeply insecure, a result of its incomplete democratic consolidation. It had not undergone a full historical reckoning. It never really had the chance, since the country's peaceful transition from fascism necessitated amnesia about the past so as not to risk stirring old ghosts. It was a pact of forgetting. But by not addressing the past, Spain would always be haunted by it. "It's sort of a paradox," Esperanza observed. "Going forward depends on looking backward."

Our wide-ranging discussion inevitably touched on American politics, and I responded without inhibition, expressing in fragmented Spanish deep dismay with the country's turn. My fiery condemnation even surprised me. Bafflement with the country's direction, unbeknownst to me, had evolved into a fierce anger that, given the opportunity, erupted with ferocity. "Fuck the place," I said in a moment of rage. Then I apologized. "I guess I didn't realize how frustrated I am."

Esperanza would not have it, pointing out that such passion was laudable. "There's nothing worse than apathy," she said. Alex momentarily came to mind. Was he apathetic or cynical? Did he truly not care that he worked at a bank implicated in the economic crisis, or did he merely present a casual façade to justify it? Which was worse? I had no idea.

We continued chatting for a while longer before Esperanza announced she had to leave on account of a dinner engagement. We bundled up and made our way together to the subway, where I bade her farewell. When I embraced her, she clutched me for an interval longer than I anticipated. I was not sure if that reflected a cultural norm. I hoped not.

Later that night, the train whistle once again intruded on my sleep, shrieking across the high desert plain, prompting familiar panic as I picked up the pace along the tracks. On this occasion, though the train whistle periodically brayed like a wounded animal, the steam engine itself never appeared from the heat ripples lofting up on the plain. I hurried along double-time, regardless.

CHAPTER 13

BRINKMANSHIP

Once again playing coy, I waited several days to contact Esperanza. This time, she dispensed with cumbersome dating etiquette, responding an hour later by inviting me to join her and one of her special-needs students the following day at a contemporary art museum. I readily agreed, and we congregated midmorning at the venue, a vibrant white structure a city block long that combined straight and curved lines and was garnished with conical ornamentations and filigree.

Esperanza greeted me affectionately in front of the venue's glass façade, which resembled glass scaffolding. "I'm so happy you're joining us," she said. Having met with her editor earlier that day, she was elegantly turned out in business attire—black pants and jacket, and heels.

Elena, her student, a shy teenager with a round face and plaintive eyes, appeared unsure of how to negotiate our introduction. "It's a pleasure to meet you," I said heartily in Spanish, trying to put her at ease. She bowed her head shyly and mumbled something inaudible.

"Don't worry," Esperanza interposed, "he's nicer than he looks."

This seemed to do the trick, as Elena giggled, and she did so again when I corrected Esperanza. "What she meant to say," I said, "is I'm very nice looking."

The museum's interior, also blindingly white, had a futuristic feel, with cylindrical columns, elevated walkways, and a sunlit atrium. We bought tickets and strolled through the first exhibition, an assemblage of vacuum cleaners, some mounted on black pedestals, others suspended from the ceiling. One was floating in a tank of water. An adjoining room, featuring installments by the same artist, who apparently had a strange appliance fetish, abounded with washing machines and dryers, again mounted creatively.

The three of us proceeded to the second floor to the museum's showpiece, a shimmering ten-foot sculpture in metallic blue resembling a dog made from sausage-shaped balloons. A museum brochure stated cryptically that the piece "personified the boundless ambition and dissipation that both edify and defame the postindustrial global landscape." Dozens of delighted museum-goers happily buzzed about the piece, taking selfies. By contrast, Elena, gazing at the oversized canine, shrugged in confusion.

At our own pace, we moseyed separately through a dozen more galleries on the top floor before reuniting for lunch in the museum's café. Nibbling on a salad, Elena expressed confusion. "I don't know what I'm going to say," she remarked, referencing the school project that had prompted the museum visit. "I just don't get any of it."

Esperanza offered consolation. "There's nothing to get. There's no hidden meaning here. Trying to find it only makes you dumber.

"Look at Leev," she added. "He's been attempting to make heads or tails of it, and as a result, his Spanish has gotten even worse. He'll be mute if we stay here much longer!"

Elena and I laughed.

"Don't worry, Pretty," Esperanza said, patting Elena's head tenderly, "we'll work on your paper together. We can bullshit as well as this place. You've got nothing to worry about."

Elena smiled appreciatively.

We took in the final wing and its featured collection of bicycles that were welded together and arranged into various geometric forms. We departed, neither enlightened nor particularly moved.

"I hope that didn't set back your Spanish too much, Leev" Elena joked.

This prompted Esperanza to add, "It can't get much worse!"

After Elena departed, Esperanza and I roamed about, as Esperanza said she needed to clear her head. Switching from playful to pensive, she said her editor was concerned about the progress of her investigative report on migrant labor. Her lack of hard evidence jeopardized the piece. She explained that she was having trouble linking several prominent regional politicians to their suspected benefactors—companies in the region reliant on the foreign workers.

I humbly suggested how she might revive the report, but mostly I listened attentively, allowing Esperanza to unburden herself. Being a journalist for a paper operating on a razor's edge, she said, was stressful. You were only as good as your next piece, regardless of your body of work and its collective merit.

Esperanza apologized for dominating the conversation and

attempted to redirect. I fended her off, expressing empathy for her frustration about her job insecurity.

The discussion took a turn when we ducked into a café. Esperanza opined about her professional future. Maybe, she said wistfully, she could find work at a bigger news media outlet, perhaps in Madrid. The problem was that the industry was hemorrhaging. Jobs in the field were being cut, not created. I offered consolation. Getting one's professional ducks in a row was difficult. I knew this well. My own job in New York was well compensated, but it lacked purpose. I was just a corporate cog. Most of my friends had fared no better. One or two had jobs they enjoyed, but they were the exception that proved the rule. Most were unhappy. By contrast, I noted, she was not doing badly. She was passionate about her work, and its potential to have a positive impact was enormous. That was rare. My words seemed to raise Esperanza's spirits. She thanked me.

I accompanied Esperanza to her bus stop and, when she turned to face me, expressed my gratitude for her invitation. My eyes locked with hers, causing me to lose my train of thought. "I… appreciate you…for," I muttered, skidding to a clumsy falloff. I couldn't take my eyes off her and I couldn't think. She was looking directly back into my eyes. We stood face-to-face in silence for what seemed like forever. Recognizing my feebleness, Esperanza slowly leaned in and kissed me gently me on the lips.

I did not react. Nothing. I didn't close my eyes as she neared. I didn't cock my head or pucker my lips as hers met mine. I just stood there slack-jawed in wide-eyed disbelief.

Esperanza pulled back. "I'm sorry, Leev. I just thought…" embarrassed, she struggled for words.

"I thought…you were, well…with the Italian guy, Frangelico."

"Ha!" she smiled, " Do you mean Francesco? No, silly, we broke up a long time ago."

It was the magic green light to proceed. Awakened from my haze, I leaned in and, softly clutching her hands, whispered, "You're beautiful." I then kissed her deeply.

Though Spaniards exhibit few romantic inhibitions in public, our amorous display generated a few muffled snickers from several onlookers at the bus stop. Esperanza, momentarily embarrassed, reverted to hugging me. We stood in gentle repose, silently embracing on the sidewalk, for several minutes—or maybe longer. Time didn't have much meaning in this moment.

"I liked you the moment I saw you," I whispered in English into Esperanza's ear, not entrusting the conveyance of such a vital sentiment to my lousy Spanish.

"Me too," Esperanza replied in English.

The next day at work, I had trouble hiding my feelings, prompting inquiries. "Yanqui, you look very happy with yourself," Andres playfully observed as I donned an apron at the beginning of my shift. "Have you helped overthrow a government? Or maybe killed a dissident?"

"No, of course not," I parried. "I'm looking forward to poisoning a few of my colleagues, though."

Belen also picked up on my mood. Unable to suppress my delight, I told her about Esperanza, whom she recalled from the party. She expressed surprise, recalling that a male companion, whom she'd assumed was her boyfriend, had accompanied Esperanza in the plaza.

I assured her Esperanza was single. "Besides," I explained, "once she learned that I'm a successful dishwasher, she couldn't resist."

That evening, I breezily dispensed with my kitchen duties in high spirits and eagerly returned home to email Esperanza about getting together the following day for lunch. We met at a café across town in a gritty neighborhood.

Esperanza, dressed in elegant business attire, once again was preoccupied with her faltering investigative report that, she said, would be dropped if she could not produce hard evidence supporting her suspicion of a conspiracy between the regional authority and textile manufactures to exploit workers. Guillermo, her editor, was adamant. She had to deliver soon—or else.

"It's so frustrating! Roadblocks have been placed before me, naturally—powerful interests don't want this story getting out. But normally I have some angle, some means. This time, nothing."

I attempted to offer comfort, expressing my expectation that eventually the wall of silence would crack. Somebody would cough up details. Esperanza smiled and, apparently hoping to change the topic, inquired as to my job. When I responded flippantly, she asked whether I had spoken with my parents of late.

"No, not lately. What are you doing the rest of the day?"

She flashed an exasperated gaze. We continued to chat about frivolities for fifteen minutes before she excused herself on account of a pending meeting. "Thank you for meeting me," she said indifferently. We kissed coldly and parted ways.

Our following two meetings, both between her work engagements, unfolded the same way. I assumed a carefree air to attempt to offset her work-related angst. It didn't work. Esperanza appeared to resent my casual responses to her questions about myself, as if my lighthearted comportment indicated I was not taking her own struggles with sufficient gravity. Yet when I did precisely that by keenly inquiring about her job, she replied frivolously, eager to change the subject. I was at a loss. It seemed I could do no right.

Esperanza was slipping away.

My hunches were correct. Two weeks after our first kiss and two days after our last lackluster meeting, Esperanza called me just as I was leaving class and suggested we link up at a bar in my neighborhood. She sounded glum.

When I arrived, Esperanza was seated in a booth at the bar's back end. She rose and feebly embraced me. "Hi," she said coldly.

"What's wrong?" I responded, getting right to the point. "Did something happen at work?"

"No," she said. "Everything's fine. Well, not fine. The same as always."

"Your editor didn't kill the story?"

"No, but he probably will. Guillermo is great. We get along well, but he's under a lot of pressure to produce results. And so am I."

"Oh," I replied, sensing that the shoe was about to drop.

It was.

A waiter took our order, after which Esperanza remarked, "Leev, I don't think this is working."

I knew it was coming, but the words still stung—deeply. My throat constricted.

"It just isn't," Esperanza added solemnly. "I'm sorry."

"Is it that guy—you know, the one in the plaza?"

Esperanza squinted in confusion. "What?" she asked. "What are you talking about?" She seemed genuinely resentful.

"You know, that guy. Are you with him? Is that why?"

"Sergio?"

"I guess."

"No," she shot back bitterly. "I told you already, we're not together. We never were. I don't even like him. He's a friend of a friend. Nothing more."

"I don't understand," I replied meekly. "I thought…"

Esperanza, looking frustrated, paused as the waiter set down on the table two cups of tea.

"There's no one else. Leev," she said with irritation. "Granted, I'm going through a difficult time at work, so I'm not in the best frame of mind...but you're, well, impossible."

"Impossible?" I repeated, puzzled. "How?"

"You've told me practically nothing about yourself. You ask about me whenever I ask about you, to escape all scrutiny. I've never met anyone so secretive—and I'm a journalist! I know nothing about your parents, past relationships, or anything, really. You're a mystery. Behind that wall you've created there's someone I want to know. You're obviously passionate about politics. You briefly revealed that at La Boqueria. And your quitting a corporate job in New York suggests there's more to you than you let on. But all that is inaccessible. I don't want to be with a robot, Leev. I want a living, breathing human—someone capable of intimacy, capable of being loved and giving loved. Why would I waste my time otherwise?"

Esperanza's indictment stung. I sat stunned and motionless, like a deer rounding a hedge and finding itself face-to-face with a wolf.

"I'm sorry," I uttered, my voice breaking. "I didn't mean it." What 'it' referenced, I was not exactly sure. The words just dribbled out. It was reflexive.

Esperanza stared at me impassively, as if awaiting a credible explanation. None was forthcoming. I was dumbfounded. I had no idea what to say. Esperanza shook her head and reached for her purse. "I should go." She placed a few bills on the table for her untouched tea.

Life's arc is shaped by a handful of inflection points that determine its ultimate trajectory. An action taken or not taken, an opportunity seized or missed—these are what define the path our lives follow. What we call "destiny" is simply that which flows from our own response to such flashpoint events.

Here, in a nondescript café in a hardscrabble Barcelona neighborhood, I confronted a life-altering moment. I felt it in my bones. My presence in Spain and, perhaps, my very presence itself, made no sense without Esperanza. She was my "destiny." If she departed, I would never see her again. This I knew.

With an assertion of will that surprised even me, I stood and grabbed Esperanza's arm as she stood to leave. The forceful intervention took her aback, and she turned and gazed at me with fearful expectation.

"I need you," I pleaded in English, peering into her eyes intently. "I need you…to give me another chance. Please."

Esperanza's defensive posture transformed; her astonished look morphed into one of sympathy, and her shoulders fell. Yet, she merely nodded subtly and, once released from my grasp, pivoted and left.

Hours later, I left her a voice mail apologizing for my forceful and pathetic display. I waited tremulously for a response. None came. I called again the next morning and kept my phone on me at work in order to not miss any incoming calls. As I was removing my soaked smock at closing, Esperanza sent me a text offering to meet the following day. I could think of nothing else during my sleepless night.

Esperanza alighted from a bus at Plaça de Catalunya in the early afternoon casually dressed in khaki pants and a sweater. Her expression was impossible to determine, as she was wearing sunglasses. When I approached, she smiled lukewarmly and hugged me wanly, saying nothing when I thanked her for meeting me. It was sunny, so I suggested we walk down the Rambla.

As we ambled stiffly down the busy boulevard side by side, palpably separated by an unseen barrier, I avoided light banter, instead launching into a candid English-Spanish hodgepodge confessional, beginning with my decision to leave my job in New York. What did I have to lose?

I told Esperanza of my errant hope that a corporate job would provide a measure of fulfillment unrealized as a government paper pusher buried in the bowels of a bureaucracy. The topical work at a prestigious consultancy required intellectual nimbleness, I explained, yet ultimately it was to inform the investment decisions of large corporations about whose fate I cared little.

A job could not be "good" if it did no good. It could only be a means to make ends meet. And toxic office politics that rewarded shameless pandering and cloying deference were lethal. Eventually, having lost confidence in the purpose and logic of my so-called career, I had abandoned it.

I told Esperanza about my lousy past relationships, including Gita, whose profound self-absorption was frustratingly typical. The women I dated, I recounted, were parasitic. They sought hosts, not partners. Their ambition was their ambition. There were exceptions, of course, but those with tender and kind dispositions tended to lack emotional depth, spark. They were boring. Dating was a crushing game. I had tired of it.

I told Esperanza of my mother and father and their nomadic

lives. They marched around the country in service of my father's quest for professional fulfillment, but it was a fool's errand, as formal structures like academia were anathema to him. Both he and my mother were decent people, but self-absorption constrained their virtue. I described a dream in which my father, deciding that heaven was too regimented, decamped for hell, taking my mother and me with him. "Growth flows from adversity," he yelled as we descended into the inferno.

I told Esperanza of the noxious political climate corroding America. I had once assumed the Right wing's slide toward authoritarianism eventually would run its course, as the country's democratic tradition simply would not abide it. No longer. The rise of the Patriot Posse and its founder, the crass radio personality, dashed my hopes. Lies were presented as truth and truth dismissed as lies. Hate was the currency of the realm. The scales had fallen from my eyes. America was not exceptional. It was lucky—until now.

Mine was a black portrait. It could not be otherwise: the world, my world, was a dark, cynical place. It was also a hidden world, obscured by a carefully constructed facade of disarming irreverence and charm. Whenever threatened with revelation, I adroitly redirected conversational topics back at my interlocutor. It was an easy enough parlor trick, since most people are profoundly egotistical.

The self-introspection revealed a wasted core within. Esperanza, for her part, remained oddly quiet as we walked the length of the Rambla to the monument to Columbus, and then to the beach near the former Olympic village. With her eyes hidden by sunglasses, I could not surmise her reaction to my nihilistic rant, but I assumed she was horrified. What other reaction was possible?

After we had walked up and down the beach promenade, the sun began to set. We turned and headed back in the direction we'd come. Esperanza remained quiet, even after I fell silent, having exhausted myself from the ruthless unburdening. We walked for some time without saying a word. I interpreted this as Esperanza's disapproval. She did not like what she heard. How could she?

As we neared a stretch between the beach and Barri Gòtic, I plotted my next move. When we reached the following block, I would offer to accompany Esperanza to the Rambla, where she could catch a bus home. Once there, I would thank her for her company and bid her farewell. It was the only means of salvaging any dignity after my miserable venting.

However, as we turned a corner past a series of outdoor market stalls, Esperanza, without saying a word, took hold of my hand. It was the simplest of gestures, the bridging of a physical chasm measured in inches. Yet I knew instantaneously, as I had known days earlier in the café when Esperanza had made for the door, that my life would be forever changed, only this time for the better.

Esperanza would be mine.

I wondered what redeeming value she saw in the person before her, a drifter with no job prospects, no family, no future. The drifter's easygoing, carefree exterior had appeal, I assumed, but the rot within could not. It could only shock and repel. Yet Esperanza had demanded entry and, once exposed, was not repulsed. I was confused.

We continued another block without exchanging words. When we neared the side streets leading to the Barri Gòtic,

Esperanza took off her sunglasses and said, "Let's go to your place." I nodded silently.

We walked hand-in-hand through the Barri Gòtic, whose medieval buildings cast hypnotic shadows on its serpentine streets as dusk fell. When we arrived at my building, I produced the skeleton key and, turning the latch to my heavy door, ushered Esperanza through it into the darkened vestibule and up to the third floor and into my apartment.

Esperanza, still holding my hand, made a slow loop around the place, like a detective at a crime scene. Then facing me, she observed, "I like it. It's charming," after which she tugged on my hand and pulled me toward the bedroom. When we crossed the threshold, she pivoted and, without saying a word, kissed me.

Moments later, she nestled her head in the crook of my neck and embraced me tightly. We stood enrapt in each other's arms, curiously saying nothing for several minutes, like reunited lovers. Eventually, Esperanza undid my shirt. I reciprocated. Between passionate kisses, we undressed each other with zealous clumsiness and fell into bed.

CHAPTER 14

THE METAMORPHOSIS

Over the ensuing six weeks, Esperanza and I achieved a certain pleasant domesticity as, effectively, she moved in with me. Shuttling between my place and hers, a cluttered shoebox across town shared with two roommates, made no sense. On weekday mornings, we went our separate ways. She went to one of her jobs, I went to my language class followed by the restaurant. Each evening we happily reunited and, on the weekends, we never parted.

Our relationship's rapid evolution felt natural. We reveled in each other's company, for me in unanticipated ways. Spending time with past girlfriends had been something I'd done out of a sense of obligation, like eating vegetables, since I got little out of it. On occasion, the task might unexpectedly surprise and pay dividends, but all too often it was a labored chore done for some unarticulated sense of obligation.

Spending time with Esperanza was no sacrifice. On the contrary. I enjoyed every minute I spent with her. Her insight and caring were a source of fascination and comfort. They empowered me. She empowered me. Thus I felt vacant and wan without her, as that experienced together was far more vibrant and vivid than that done alone. It was an empowering and completely novel sensation.

It also was thrilling to be liberated from the artifices separating the person I was from the person I presented myself to be. I seldom revealed the authentic person residing behind the artificial constructs, since few sought an introduction to him or, in my judgment, were worthy of one.

This was all well and good, for the most part, except when it came to the matter of achieving emotional intimacy, which demands authenticity. One cannot, after all, fall in love with a persona. It has to be the genuine article. And the litmus test for being genuine is being vulnerable.

Since Esperanza required I dispense with phony personas, in a curious way, being with her allowed me to be with myself, my true self. And once that authentic self emerged, I realized how much I enjoyed inhabiting him. As a consequence, I steered clear of returning to my counterfeit cocoon when not absolutely necessary.

Practical considerations soon intruded on my newfound commitment to authenticity. Having sought exile in Spain nearly five months earlier, the expiration of my six-month tourist visa, which I had already extended once, was nearing. I could, of course, overstay the visa without immediate consequence. Javier and Andres and many others did precisely that. It was common.

Yet it also was problematic. In addition to living in chronic fear of being found out and repatriated, lacking legal status would jeopardize my ability to return to Spain whenever I did leave, foreclosing my ability to return home, even for a brief vacation. Nor would I be able to obtain a work permit, if the opportunity ever arose. It would seal my fate. I needed a better option.

I had not contemplated the matter, or much else of consequence, when I'd departed for Spain, since my plans were little more than a careless improvisation. In any case, I anticipated running low on money around the time my visa expired, so questions about my eventual legal status abroad were irrelevant. Working at the restaurant altered the equation, however, as I could now afford to stay in Spain much longer than anticipated.

Mostly, though, Esperanza altered the equation. Our relationship was new, yet it had quickly gained utmost consequence. Nothing mattered more. I could not fathom life without Esperanza and therefore could not fathom leaving Spain. The two were inextricably linked.

Some research online provided a potential solution: return to New York before my visa expired and, once there, apply for a new passport under the false pretense of having lost my old one. A new passport with a new identification number could allow me to reset the clock when I reentered Spain—at least in theory.

European immigration authorities were no fools, of course. They knew all the many ways people tried to game the system, including far more elaborate ruses than I could even imagine. But my plan was not unrealistic, either. Spanish customs were famously inept, particularly with respect to electronic record keeping. The scandal-prone immigration department was constantly making news. Moreover, as an American, I was bound to face less scrutiny than other would-be entrants or darker-skinned arrivals from Latin America and the Middle East, not to mention Africa. Consequently, I figured my chances were fairly good.

I tentatively made plans to fly to New York near the end of the month, around the time Esperanza planned to visit her family in Madrid. But before I finalized arrangements, I received an email from my headhunter, who had gone quiet ever since I informed him that, given my present residence in Spain, I was interested in exceptional opportunities only.

He wrote of a vacancy at a bank in London. The research-oriented position, located within striking distance of Spain, potentially was a good match for me, drawing on my experience at Marshall Cooper and in Washington. The bank had seen my resume and was interested. He asked whether I wanted to pursue it.

I had fled the corporate workplace, with its artificiality and amorality, promising never to return. I could not stomach the notion. What's more, donning the fabricated persona required to survive such a circumstance ran counter to my newfound commitment to authenticity. Yet principles have a price—one I could not afford.

I was in an unsustainable state of limbo. Happy as I was free of the corporate workplace, I was in a race against time. With my savings drawing down and my legal standing in Spain in jeopardy, the status quo could not hold. Nor could it for other reasons.

The gritty restaurant work had proven unexpectedly enjoyable, as I valued the camaraderie of my unpretentious colleagues and the unexpected sense of accomplishment derived from manual labor. But I could relish the experience precisely because it was temporary. The lack of deep fulfillment from washing dishes one day to the next eventually would become crippling. It was only a matter of time.

What was more, the inevitable self-loathing that would result would imperil my relationship with Esperanza. That "hurt people hurt people" may be a Hollywood cliché, but it is true. I could not at once dislike myself and have a full relationship, regardless of how tolerant Esperanza might be.

Boxed into a corner, I responded affirmatively to the head-hunter and promptly set up an interview in London. The excursion, which would be covered by a stipend offered by the bank, also would allow me to acquire a new passport at the U.S. embassy, thus negating the need to return to New York. It might not solve all my problems, but it was my best shot under the circumstances. I had no viable alternative.

For a few days, I did not tell Esperanza of the latest turn of events, given their implications, or the likelihood that our fledgling relationship would become long distance were I to move to London. But I could not hold out. Eventually, I fessed up, laying out my reasoning for pursuing the opportunity.

Esperanza offered support for my decision, but I could tell it rattled her. "I hope you get the job," she offered unconvincingly. That evening, while we lay in bed, she broke down in tears suddenly, blaming stress over her failing investigative report. I knew otherwise. We both feared the future.

The following week, I departed Barcelona on an uncharacteristically overcast morning, landing two and a half hours later on a characteristically overcast London afternoon. I made my way to my hotel with a small carry-on and garment bag for the one suit that I had brought with me to Spain, prepared to undergo an artificial transformation from disgruntled corporate outcast to eager financial-sector pledge.

The following morning, I unzipped the garment bag nervously and slipped on the musty jacket and pants as though I were donning a wet suit in preparation to swim in shark-infested waters. The tie felt like a noose, the black dress shoes, cement boots.

Outside the hotel, I bought a newspaper featuring an alarming headline about Schmidt's latest primary win, and took a taxi to the U.S. embassy, where I applied for a new passport under the guise of having left my old one in a taxi. A new document, the friendly consular official assured, would be ready the following afternoon, well ahead of my flight the next day.

From central London, I hailed another taxi to Canary Wharf. Graced with an impressive skyline of gleaming glass office towers, the East London area served as a nerve center for global finance, rivaled in importance only by Wall Street. In its hallowed capitalist grounds, tens of thousands plied their trade, occasionally creating wealth but more often recklessly destroying it.

As the cabbie, a Bangladesh-born Briton, complained bitterly in a nearly inscrutable South Asian accent about immigrants ruining the country, I felt my stomach knot. Approaching our destination, beads of cold sweat formed on my forehead. I began to shiver. My discomfort with the entire undertaking was being manifested corporally.

Fortunately, I was running twenty minutes early, so I asked the cabbie to pull over at a coffee shop and dashed to its bathroom. I threw water over face, loosened my tie, and, barricading myself in a stall, closed my eyes and took deep breaths, exhaling through pursed lips. I did this for a few minutes, focusing intently on the pastoral mental image of a countryside.

An ability to wow in interviews is one of my superpowers. I could, at a moment's notice, access the supremely confident persona of a foot soldier ready for battle in the corporate trenches. My over-the-top impression—intolerably obnoxious and pathologically cocksure—bordered on parody, but it worked. I had gotten the job at Marshall Cooper over six other final candidates, including two with doctorates, on the basis of my outstanding performance in front of the firm's principals. Summoning my corporate alter ego had never been a problem in the past, but it was today.

Indeed, on this day, my superpowers were the source of my anxiety, as I feared the implications of acing the interview. My body was viscerally reacting to the prospect of returning to the corporate realm I so detested. It was as though I were a traumatized veteran returning to the bloody battlefields—a kind of post-traumatic stress disorder.

But return I must. I had no choice. Any worthwhile future included Esperanza, and the only way to ensure that was to secure this job.

A calm descended over me during my impromptu meditation in the bathroom stall. My shoulders fell, and my breathing flattened out. I stopped sweating. At last I was at peace. Once sufficiently composed, I exited the bathroom and, girding myself, made my way toward the glass tower.

To my relief, with each step in the fresh air, my superpowers returned: I grew more invigorated, as though adrenaline were being injected directly into my veins. I came alive, furiously. I felt hot and restless. By the time I reached the building's entrance, my entire body—pectorals, abdominals, fists—was pulsating with the aggrieved tension of a gladiator preparing for mortal combat. Violent thoughts raced through my head. I was ready for battle. Bring it on!

The transformation was complete.

The existentially conflicted dishwasher had been vanquished. In his place was a scandalously self-assured and unprincipled financier ready to do whatever was necessary to win. In this testosterone-addled guise, I felt capable of shamelessly hawking shitty subprime securitized mortgages or worthless junk bonds, consequences be damned. Or just beating someone up. I was a Master of the Universe.

The glass leviathan's pink marble interior had a massive atrium, in the center of which was a duplicate of the metallic sculpture resembling the sausage-shaped balloon dog prominently displayed in Barcelona's contemporary art museum, only this one was red, not blue. It looked sublime. It was a modern marvel, a work of genius. I made a mental note to visit its twin in Barcelona.

"We've been looking forward to your arrival, Mr. Ackerman," said an attractive blond receptionist sitting behind a large desk when I presented myself after alighting on the forty-fifth floor. "I will tell Mr. Cooper you're here. Kindly wait there." She pointed to a small sitting area.

With my leg bouncing furiously to release excessive energy, I sat on a leather couch, imploring myself to fight the urge to throttle each person that walked by. The slightest provocation, I feared, might tip me over the edge.

"Livingstone, I presume?" a voice said, interrupting my internal dialogue. The salutation approximated that supposed utterance by journalist Henry Morton Stanley upon finally encountering my namesake, David Livingstone, who had disappeared into Africa's interior. It had been repeated to me countless times. I usually cringed on such occasions. It did not bother me this time. It even sounded pleasant.

"Jack?" I asked, referencing the principal contact with whom my headhunter had put me in contact.

"Yes, it's pleasure to meet you," he replied. "Thanks for coming."

Jack looked roughly my age. Medium height and skinny, he had hooded brown eyes and bulbous nose, along with a sloping chin that was like an exclamation point on his face. His medley of unusual facial features gave him a slightly menacing countenance that, if encountered on a dark street corner, might prompt the prudent pedestrian to cross to the other side.

As striking as his looks was his attire. His perfectly tailored dark pin-striped suit hugged his torso and was elegantly complemented by a royal blue shirt, monogrammed on the sleeves, and a bright yellow tie held in place with a silver clip. On his feet were black loafers so shiny that they looked as though they had been polished with an industrial buffer. Around his wrist was a watch with large Roman numerals and leather strap. His fingernails glimmered like manicured oval ice cubes.

I wanted to punch him.

"Please, follow me," Jack said, leading me through a door, past an open area lined with cubicles populated with impeccably dressed bankers peering at upright displays. While chitchatting about the weather, we turned a corner and through the door of a rectangular conference room with a large mahogany table, around which were roughly a dozen leather chairs. Several canvases with splotches of splattered paint—art, apparently—adorned the walls.

"Anywhere you'd like," Jack offered amiably. "Make yourself comfortable while I retrieve Marsha and Crispin." I sat in the middle of the table, surpassing a storm of twitches and tics, wondering how I was going to sit still for the interview's duration.

Minutes later, Jack returned with two sharply dressed colleagues, a statuesque middle-aged woman with blond hair and thin face and a stocky man with a receding hairline, also appearing to be in his forties.

"Marsha Wallace," the woman said, holding out her hand. "It's a pleasure to meet you. Many thanks for coming all this way."

"The pleasure is mine," I answered in a self-assured timbre, inadvertently shaking her hand with excessive firmness, prompting her to subtly wince. I turned and exchanged pleasantries with Crispin, who warmly patted me on the shoulder as we shook hands. I fought the urge to twist his arm until it cracked.

"We're delighted to meet you," Marsha began, motioning me to take a seat.

"We generally recruit locally, by which I mean in Europe. We do, of course, have a global reach, so our employees come from all over. However, integrating talent from overseas can be difficult for administrative reasons, so generally we seek to place new hires in regional hubs associated with their places of origin. This is standard practice in the industry, though, like I said, many exceptions exist. I have indispensible colleagues on my team from Tokyo and Singapore, respectively. In normal circumstances, our HR here in London would have routed your CV to our regional headquarters in New York. But your background caught our attention, and after learning of your current residency in Spain, we decided to reach out to you."

I nodded and, finding it impossible to suppress my overweening desire to hold forth, took the interview's reins. "Thank you, Marsha, and to you, Michael and Crispin," I announced, my leg, hidden beneath the tabletop, now bouncing madly. "I'm delighted to meet all of you too. I recognize that I may be a nontraditional candidate, at least with respect to how I came to your attention, but I hope to turn that to my advantage."

Seeking to dispense promptly with the question on my interrogators' minds, I explained the circumstances of my being in Spain, and my having honored an agreement with my fiancée, a Spanish journalist, to return to Barcelona after years together in New York. It simply would have been unfair to do otherwise.

It had been a difficult decision nevertheless, I said. I was thriving at Marshall Cooper. The work was rewarding and the monetary compensation superb. Senior management was assured. But I did not regret my decision. "Character is destiny," I stated, offering up an observation that normally would have turned my stomach. "I believe this to my core. It pertains to one's personal and public relationships alike. You can't compartmentalize these things. I had made a commitment to my fiancée, and I was not going to back out on it. That's who I am."

My fiancée, I went on, was now working freelance and thus not bound to Barcelona. She could live anywhere in Europe. The sabbatical forced on me by circumstance had been worthwhile, but I was now ready to return to the workforce.

Brilliant Brad, I knew, would verify my bogus tale. I already had alerted him about my being in Spain, not California as I had claimed when I left Marshall Cooper, and received assurance he would vouch for a contrived narrative explaining my sudden departure from the firm.

I pivoted seamlessly, delving into my accomplishments, real but mostly embellished, at Marshall Cooper. By my description, I was a veritable genius whose passion and dedication were the envy of my colleagues, not a modestly dedicated drone secretly burning with resentment. I also detailed my tenure in Washington, again presenting myself as a prodigy rather than anonymous bureaucrat itching for a change.

I peppered my flamboyant sales pitch with five-star words like "perspicacious" and "maladroit," along with nauseating business jargon tucked away for the occasion. It was a frighteningly polished performance.

Crispin thanked me for my thorough recital and then queried me about my quantitative background, as the job would require significant economic analysis. I was ready. I threw back at him a host of software packages on which I was an expert. It was, like everything out of my mouth, an exaggeration, if not an outright lie, but it seemed to go over well.

Jack, taking his turn, threw a curveball of his own. Which markets, he asked, faced elevated risk? And how could the financial sector mitigate them?

Alex, whom I had consulted ahead of the interview, promised I was likely to be asked questions about present market conditions, or some variation thereof. It was standard practice. I was ready.

Cribbing off an internal report Alex's firm had produced on the continued vulnerability of the Latin American real estate market's post-economic crisis, a report that Alex had provided and that I virtually had committed to memory, I launched into a scholarly oration, citing impressively arcane indicators as to why land was still overvalued in Argentina and Uruguay.

Crispin and Marsha exchanged awed glances. Who was this ringer? their expressions betrayed.

I continued uninterrupted for fifteen magisterial minutes, my leg still bouncing furiously, before seguing into another long soliloquy about wasteful infrastructure spending in Japan and the country's overleveraged banks, other topics for which Alex had furnished the background.

When I finished, Jack, stammering slightly, uttered, "Well, that was very, very informative. The breadth of that analysis, that is. If I may, how did you come by all that?"

It was, I explained, residual knowledge gained during my tenure at Marshall Cooper. I apologized with false humility for the purportedly dated information, which, in fact, was current. "I've been out of the game for some months."

The interview took another predictable turn when Jack asked me customary interview questions: What are your strengths and weaknesses? Give an example of a challenge you encountered and how you overcame it. Where do you see yourself in five years?

I knocked these out the park too.

Marsha thanked me for my candor and, turning to her two other colleagues, suggested Nigel join us. Nigel, she explained, one of the bank's senior executives, was director for investment banking. I surmised he was summoned only when job candidate received the imprimatur of his subordinates.

Marsha departed and returned ten minutes later with a tall man in a pin-striped three-piece suit and shockingly orange tie. Nigel had an exceptionally thin face, small brown eyes, and long, narrow nose on whose tip was perched a pair of rimless bifocals. His gray hair was a bit unkempt, and his blue shirt had creases, as if it had been reworn without ironing.

He held out his hand and said, with an impeccably posh British accent instantly identifying him as an aristocrat in hopelessly class-bound Britain, "Livingstone, it is a delight to meet you. Marsha relayed that you have made quite the impression."

With violent fantasies still swirling in my head, I imagined incapacitating the pretentious twit, who reminded me of Mortimer from Marshall Cooper, with a kick in the groin, and then snapping sycophant Marsha's neck like a carrot stick. I might have a chance to take out Jack and Crispin before Nigel could react.

If so, I'd double back and strangle the arrogant bastard with his ridiculous tie.

It would be close.

"Same here," I answered, shaking Nigel's hand, again too firmly.

Nigel sat down at the head of the table, displacing Marsha, who deposited herself to his left. "I understand you've told Marsha, Jack, and Crispin about your background, Livingstone, so it would be unfair to prevail on you to repeat it. I trust that they can relay the key takeaways.

"Instead, allow me to tell you about our work, which might help you determine whether this would be a good match for you. I say this because we believe our people are our greatest asset. They're our value add. But that is only possible when we have the right people, and that, in turn, necessitates we attract top-flight talent."

Nigel proceeded to drone on about bank's commitment to its staff, which rang hollow given that, during the height of the financial crisis, it had fired hundreds of low- and midlevel workers while simultaneously doling out extravagant bonuses to its executive staff.

I was nearly ready to rocket out of my seat and slap the pompous suit when he finally wrapped up. I repeated my glib speech citing my credentials, paring it down to its essentials, and then offered up a toadying homily about high finance. "Risk management is particularly critical given market instability," I added, "and will only became more so if the Labour Party comes to power."

My audience erupted in hilarity.

"Well, Livingstone, I can see why Marsha sang your praises. I'm impressed. I think I can safely say we're all very impressed."

Nigel continued with the niceties, but my mind was preoccupied with assessing how best to murder the four with a ballpoint pen. Somehow, I managed to maintain my composure for the interview's remaining minutes, smiling and nodding when appropriate. I deserved an offer based on the remarkable self-restraint that kept my inner Mr. Hyde from overwhelming my outward Dr. Jekyll.

While shepherding me to the elevator, Jack asked how I was occupying my time in Barcelona. Perhaps overconfident by my rhapsodic display in the boardroom, I replied I was working in a restaurant, and when Jack sought elaboration, I explained that I washed dishes. The confession elicited wrinkled-nose confusion.

"Really?" Jack asked incredulously. "Why would you do that?"

I beat a hasty retreat, recognizing my error. It was, I explained, just a way to kill time, implying the work was beneath me—*very* beneath me. "There's nothing to it. Better than doing nothing at all."

Jack appeared unconvinced. His expression belied incredulity. "Really?" he responded. "That's unusual. That's very unusual."

"Yes," I agreed. "Keeps me busy. I'd go crazy otherwise."

"I don't see why you'd do that," he replied. "I mean, after working in New York at such a…" he trailed off.

It took my remaining willpower to refrain from jabbing the motherfucker's eye socket with his silver tie clip. "Like I said," I replied, "there's nothing to it. It's just a pastime."

"That's…" he murmured, before bidding my farewell with a limp handshake.

I bounded out of the building feeling so energized that I

elected to return to the hotel by foot despite the considerable distance. It would help me decompress. At one crosswalk, unaccustomed to traffic's direction in England, I mistakenly looked the wrong way before proceeding, causing an oncoming car to screech to a halt. When the driver held up his hands in disgust, I unleashed a barrage of curses, to the dismay of several nearby pedestrians. "Go fuck yourselves," I yelled at them.

I picked up the pace, my strides now monstrously large, though it eventually dawned on me that I was hungry. Not just hungry, but ravenous. I needed food—fast.

I ducked into a burger joint I serendipitously came across in the following block and ordered a double cheeseburger, fries, and a shake, wolfing them down with unnatural vigor. It did nothing to satiate my appetite, so I ordered another burger, and another. I would have plunked down cash for a fourth, but a line had formed, and I was eager to get moving, so I bounded back out to the street.

I again trotted double-time toward central London, passing pedestrians as if they were stationary. Forty-five minutes later, having built up a sweat, I began to feel queasy. The sensation was at first subtle but soon grew ominous. The ill-advised meal was demanding my attention.

Spotting a coffee shop, I darted into the venue frantically, shoving aside a few patrons to gain priority access to the bathroom, where the greasy meal rocketed from my stomach with such violent force I feared my pancreas might follow the chunks of undigested burger and fries that caked the toilet bowl and adjoining wall. The accompanying noise, guttural and raw, was positively reptilian.

I sat on the bathroom floor for several minutes, panting

heavily and dazed, as if I had just undergone an exorcism. Though suddenly enervated, I got to my feet, washed off, and exited the bathroom. A queue of bewildered patrons gave me wide berth as I staggered past with bits of half-digested burger and fries speckled on my coat.

The outside air felt refreshing, if suddenly cold. I bundled my coat and set back off toward central London. Gone was my vigor. My legs were now spongy and my head dizzy. My vision was slightly blurred.

Blocks later, unable to continue, I hailed a taxi and, within minutes of returning to my room, fell into a deep slumber. I awoke briefly to phone Esperanza and then slept for twelve hours, rousing midmorning feeling only marginally better.

I had hoped to take in the city on my day off, but I was too fatigued, so I stayed close to the hotel, returning twice to nap. In the late afternoon, I picked up my new passport at the U.S. embassy.

The following afternoon, I returned to Barcelona. I might have been nervous passing through customs, but I was still strangely out of sorts and approached the immigration counter calmly. It did not matter. The customs agent, distracted by the colleague with whom he was chatting, casually scanned my document, stamped it, and handed it back without making eye contact.

A week later, I received an email from the bank. "While your skills and background are impressive," the form letter read, "we have decided to move forward with a different candidate."

CHAPTER 15

THE PURSUIT OF MEANING

"Leev!" Esperanza exclaimed breathlessly into the phone. "Guess what?"

"What?" I asked.

"Oh, I'm so happy. Where are you?"

"I'm on my way home from class. What's going on?"

"Let's meet. I want to tell you in person. Oh, never mind, I'm too excited. I had a breakthrough."

"Breakthrough?"

"Yes," Esperanza replied. "You know how my investigation was going nowhere. I thought Guillermo was going to kill it. Today I was contacted unexpectedly by my source…"

"Source?"

"An official from the regional government whom I've been cultivating for months. She told me that at least three different companies have bribed senior appointees in her office. We're talking tens of thousands of euros, paid vacations, and other inducements. Can you believe that?"

"That incredible!" I said, nearly shouting. "Can she prove it?"

"Yes! She's got financial records and receipts. This proves

illicit collusion between industry and government to break the law. This is it!"

"What fantastic news! You've worked so hard on this story."

"I know! Let's meet."

We arranged to rendezvous in the Plaça Reial, a majestic plaza sprinkled with palm trees and lanterns in the heart of the Barri Gòtic, not far from my apartment. I arrived first and sat down in one of the cafés lining the plaza and waited patiently for Esperanza, who emerged after ten minutes with a companion whom I did not recognize. The two were in animated conversation. They made a lazy loop around the plaza's perimeter and, when Esperanza spotted me, approached.

"Leev," Esperanza said boisterously, kissing me. "This is Dario. He's the older brother of one of my best friends from childhood, Nuria. We practically grew up together. I just ran into him!"

Middle-aged and ruggedly handsome, Dario, who was about my height, had long brown hair speckled with traces of white and worn in a ponytail. A scraggly beard was growing on his unshaven face, which was otherwise angular, as were his nose and cheekbones. His ocher eyes radiated worldly wisdom.

Dressed in ripped jeans splattered with paint, tattered sweater, and worn boots, and carrying a rucksack over his shoulder and a small white canvas in his free hand, he looked like a bohemian archetype.

"It's a pleasure to meet you," Dario said with an outstretched hand. "Oh, I'm sorry," he added, referring to his paint-stained skin. "I'm always covered in paint. It's an occupational hazard."

Dario, a painter, lived with his wife and two young daughters in Girona, a city about an hour northeast of Barcelona. He had come into the city to pick up art supplies after dropping off a cousin at the airport and by happenstance had crossed paths with Esperanza at a bus stop.

After I introduced myself, the two childhood acquaintances joyfully recounted stories from youth, trading anecdotes about Nuria, before Esperanza, at my urging, related the day's thrilling events. The investigative report, she estimated, would take a few weeks to complete, but its first installment could appear in days. Guillermo was optimistic. He'd been in the industry for decades and had had a hand in a number of the biggest-breaking stories impacting the region over that time. He thought this one was on par with any of them. It was a big scoop. To celebrate the news, we ordered a round of drinks.

I leaned over and kissed Esperanza as Dario proposed a toast in her honor. "To my childhood friend, who grew up to be a great journalist," he said. Then he and Esperanza said together, "*Salud, pesetas y amor—y tiempo para gozarlos. To health, money, love—and time to enjoy them!*"

Esperanza laughed. She had worked so hard on the story, which had pushed to a precipice, but her efforts had paid off. I was ecstatic for her—perhaps more so than I would be for a professional breakthrough of my own. Her triumph was my triumph. It was an altogether unexpected yet welcome sensation.

"So, Liv," Dario said cheerfully, turning to me. "What brought you to Spain?"

"I'm here learning Spanish," I replied.

"You're making great progress."

"That's thanks to me," Esperanza interjected playfully. "He could barely talk, the poor mute, before we met."

"What were you doing before you came?" Dario asked.

I hesitated. I didn't want to discuss my tenure at Marshall

Cooper, which would precipitate an unwanted conversation about the reasons I quit my job. Not today. "I was working, but, well…"

"He was working as a consultant in Manhattan," Esperanza interjected again, "but he hated it. Besides, he knew he needed to come here to meet this certain somebody special."

I was relieved. Discussion avoided. "That's true," I concurred. "At some point, Dario, I'll introduce you to my landlord, Anna."

Dario and Esperanza laughed heartily.

"So you just quit?" Dario asked. "That's brave."

Dammit, I thought, here we go again. "Well, it's a bit more complicated than that."

Dario, with an earnest expression, shrugged. "Complicated?" he asked. He wasn't going to let up. This artist was tenacious.

"Yeah, very complicated."

"How so?"

"It was the political climate, too," Esperanza interposed.

"You were unhappy with the political climate?"

"Well, yes," I answered hesitantly, realizing things were spinning out of control. I had to figure an easy way out. "My country's direction is disturbing. It has been for a long time, but I thought things would eventually sort themselves out. America's democracy is firmly established. Or so I thought. Now I'm afraid we're sliding into an abyss. It feels like we're heading toward fascism."

"Those are strong words," Dario remarked. "We Spaniards know something about fascism. We endured decades of it—with America's assistance, I might add. I can see why you're worried. This Schmidt fellow is frightening. But the problem is not limited to the United States so, forgive me, but being here isn't a good solution."

"You're right," I agreed. "I'm torn between disgust for my

country and a sense of obligation to it. Depending on the day, I never want to return, or I want to return immediately and fight for it, at least in my own small way. I'm not sure if I'll ever reconcile my views. But like I said, I didn't leave only because of politics. I hated my job."

I was proud of myself. I had managed to slip the noose by truthfully explaining myself in a way that would shut down the conversation.

"That's understandable," Dario said. "It's hard to find professional fulfillment. Very hard."

"You have," Esperanza piped in, picking up the small canvas that Dario had placed beside the table.

"What sort of painting do you do?" I asked, hoping to redirect the conversation.

"Messy painting," he said, pointing to the paint stains on his pants.

"He does beautiful still lifes," Esperanza explained, "in all sorts of vibrant colors. Portraits, too. He's been painting since I was a child. I recall seeing his beautiful work around his house when I was visiting Nuria. It was clear he had talent back then."

Dario laughed. "I'm not sure about that. An artist is 'talented' if he can put food on the table. The rest are details."

"Oh, don't be so modest," Esperanza protested.

"Well, I am not sure how talented I may be—artists never know if their work has any merit, even the ones who gain recognition—but it does bring me great satisfaction," Dario said. "Anyway, Liv, you were saying you didn't like your job."

I nodded and forced a smile, even though I was irritated that the topic of conversation had returned to my job.

"You Americans, if I may be blunt, fetishize happiness. Even your Constitution places the 'pursuit of happiness' on par with life and liberty. It's misguided. It's a recipe for unhappiness."

"It was the Declaration of Independence, not the Constitution," I corrected Dario smugly, annoyed that a stranger would arrogantly pooh-pooh my professional dissatisfaction, inferring some cultural flaw. "What's wrong with pursuing happiness anyway? Should we reconcile ourselves to misery? I hated my job. My discontent was an important indicator something was wrong, and I was right to listen to it."

"That's true, Dario," Esperanza said, coming to my defense. "I'm sure your family makes you happy, as does your art. What's wrong with that?"

"Nothing. But I'm not sure it's all that important."

"Not important?" Esperanza gasped.

Dario smiled and sipped his drink. "My two girls bring me much happiness, but being a parent also is very hard. Infants cry nonstop, require changing, and interrupt sleep. They need constant attention. It's not all fun. Parents of young children, in fact, oftentimes are less happy than their childless contemporaries. Studies have shown this. Parents report being even happier watching television or eating than interacting with their kids. Some friends of mine even confess their children are most responsible for their unhappiness!"

"That's awful!" Esperanza cried. "I don't believe it. If having children is so difficult, then why do people have them in the first place?"

"Good question," replied Dario.

"You regret having them?" Esperanza inquired with horror.

"No, of course not. I love my daughters. What I'm saying is that doing anything, including having kids, because you think it'll make you happy is a mistake. Likewise, judging a job on the basis of whether it's pleasurable also is mistaken."

Esperanza and I exchanged baffled expressions. I was beginning to grow tired of the New Age artist and began to brainstorm for excuses as to why I needed to leave. He and Esperanza would be just fine catching up without me.

Dario took a deep breath. "Happiness," he continued, "is not an end in and of itself. It may be a welcome byproduct of some other undertaking but should not be a singular pursuit."

I definitely needed out. He had lost me a while back.

"Okay, start with the basics," Dario said, sensing our continued confusion. "Happiness is fleeting. Winning the lottery may induce ecstasy, but you're apt to return to your original baseline level of contentment. Likewise, suffering an injury, even a grievous one, may render you miserable in the moment, but chances are eventually you'll revert to your emotional mean.

"The problem with pursuing happiness is that it generates tension, a consequence of craving more and more of what induces only temporary pleasure, such as money, fame, sex, et cetera. As a result, no inner peace is possible. That's one of Buddhism's main insights."

"Which is why the pursuit of happiness is misguided?" I asked inadvisably, ensuring that I would have to stick around.

"Exactly!" Dario cried, slapping the table.

"What is worth pursuing then?"

"Meaning."

"Meaning?" I uttered with bewilderment.

"Yes, meaning. That's what matters. You, Liv, hated your job. You were unhappy. But you would've been able to endure it if it gave you meaning. You would've felt that your personal sacrifice was worth it. In fact, you may have even reveled in it.

"Think about it. People endure much worse—by choice! Humanitarian aid workers in war zones are one example, teachers in rotten neighborhoods another. What motivates them? Meaning. Which is why parenting is worth it, even though it's difficult. Being a mother or father lends a sense of purpose."

"But what is meaningful to one may not be to another," I responded with irritation. "It's a matter of personal opinion. Thus 'meaning' is meaningless."

"Ah, you're onto something," Dario said, again pausing in thought momentarily, "though not for the reasons you think. What gives meaning can vary but shares a common feature: it transcends the self. It's bigger than you."

"Bigger?" Esperanza asked.

"Yes, bigger."

"Why does that matter?" I asked.

"Perhaps it has something to do with death. We, unlike any other species, as far as we know, are aware of our own mortality. We know someday we'll be no more. That knowledge haunts us. Thus we seek to transcend ourselves.

"Parenting does that. We cheat death by bringing faint copies of ourselves into the world and shaping them in our own image, which provides us posterity and thus meaning.

"Other acts of selflessness do the same, allowing us to transcend the present, connecting the here and now to the hereafter. This is why we should pursue meaning, not happiness. That's what matters!"

"Wow," Esperanza gasped. "That's heavy. I think we're going to need another round." She hailed the waiter and ordered three more beers. "You obviously do some serious thinking when you're painting. Either that or smoking lots of marijuana—this sounds like the sort of thing you think about when you're high!"

Dario chuckled. Checking his watch, he said he had to get going soon, as he needed to retreat home in time to pick up his daughters from school. "I suppose, as a father who spends a lot of time in the company of seven- and nine-year-olds, I'm starved for adult conversation. I apologize. We shouldn't waste such a nice afternoon philosophizing, especially because I'm only expert on two things: mixing acrylic paint and procrastinating. That's all."

"So what gives you meaning?" Esperanza asked, brushing off Dario's invitation to change the topic.

"My daughters, of course. They're my world. And my wife. And art. None make me happy all the time. But they tie me to something larger than myself and, as a result, give me purpose."

"Even if you're right about the importance of pursuing meaning," I conceded, "it's not clear how to go about doing so."

"It's hard," Dario observed. "We're told today that no objective meaning exists; we're just an insignificant accumulation of molecules on an insignificant ball of space dust in an insignificant universe. Meanwhile, we pass much of our lives doing jobs that offer us no fulfillment—something you know about, Liv. We're misled to believe that happiness offers salvation. We're lost."

"How do we find our way?" I asked, now intrigued. "How do we find meaning?"

Dario paused while the waiter delivered our drinks. "I only know what works for me. And that's the point. Each person has to find what gives him or her meaning."

I smirked. "That makes no sense. If life has no objective

meaning, then that meaning each individual gives it by definition has no meaning, either. It's a paradox."

"Correct."

"Correct?" I asked skeptically. "I must be missing something."

"Not at all," Dario reassured. "You're quite right; our search for meaning is contradictory. Whatever meaning we give life cannot have any objective meaning, since none exists. It must be a delusion—a happy delusion, but a delusion nonetheless."

Esperanza and I pondered the puzzling notion in silence. Finally, spotting two nuns in habits meandering across the plaza, I asked, "What about them?"

"The nuns?" Dario inquired, craning his head.

"Yes, them. Is their faith a happy delusion?"

"Absolutely. But don't get me wrong. Even though I derive no meaning from religion—I am not a believer—it comprises one of the happiest delusions. After all, for two thousand years, the church sponsored much of the culture and art that has ennobled humanity—the painting, the music, the architecture. We would not have Western civilization without it. For this, we should be grateful."

"Perhaps," Esperanza retorted, "but the same 'happy delusion' that has filled museums with beautiful artifacts and concert halls with exalted melodies also is responsible for incalculable bloodshed. We Spaniards know this well. Our ancestors wantonly killed nonbelievers in the Old World before setting out to the New World to do the same, all in service of their faith. You don't have to go back that far, of course. The Church supported Franco and vice versa. The two were one and the same!

"Whatever guise it takes—Christianity, Hinduism, Islam,

Judaism—religion's record is awful. It isn't a 'happy delusion' but rather a very unhappy one!"

Dario nodded. "You're quite right," he concurred. "Religion has a lot to answer for. Because it claims divine authority, those who derive meaning from it tend to forget it's just another delusion…"

"That's precisely the point!" Esperanza said emphatically. "Religion's dogmatism is not an aberration. It's central to it. It is, after all, the height of arrogance to believe one knows God's will, much less that God even exists. Such conceit is the opposite of the humility associated with 'happy delusions,' as described by you, which is why religion has such a terrible historical record. It's inherently self-righteous and intolerant."

"Perhaps," Dario conceded. "Yet for many people, faith provides personal comfort and peace. And it can tap into our better angels. Those two," he added, pointing to the nuns, "may well live modest lives dedicated to charitable works. They live to serve others and in return enjoy a sense of purpose. What fault can be found with that?

"My existence, however, requires that I get going soon, as my wife will kill me if I don't pick up the girls from school, and before I do that, I have to buy a few more art supplies. There you have my happy delusions—my daughters, my wife, and my art—all in one sentence!"

"So pursue meaning, not happiness, and find a happy delusion even though it's just a delusion. Is that it?" I asked.

"Correct," Dario said with a smile.

"I think you're in the wrong line of work, Dario. Forget painting. It's a waste of time. You should be running a monastery."

Dario burst out laughing.

"Oh, Liv, that's funny. Like I said, I have no great spiritual insight to offer. I only know that, after attempting for many years to find happiness by doing what I thought would make me happy, I realized I had it all backward. Like you, I was miserable. I found a new job, then another, and another, but happiness eluded me. It finally dawned on me I wasn't happy because I wasn't doing anything meaningful. And when I finally found that which gave me meaning, I realized that happiness wasn't all that important in the first place. It's actually quite simple. Don't follow your bliss. Pursue your meaning. That's all there's to it."

Dario took a final sip of his drink and attempted to place a twenty-euro note on the table, but Esperanza and I refused it. "That's very kind of you," he said, gathering his belongings. He again congratulated Esperanza and kissed her goodbye. The two promised to get together soon. To my surprise, he gave me a hearty hug, too.

"I'll be back in town soon," he remarked as he walked off. "We'll continue this then."

HAPPY DELUSION

We departed late for Valencia. The getaway came on the heels of a madcap week for Esperanza following publication of her investigative report, which kindled a media frenzy. She became a minor celebrity overnight, appearing regularly on local news programs. Esperanza was elated, as was Guillermo. He already had raised the possibility of a follow-up report on various abusive labor practices, not just those involving migrant laborers. He wanted her to begin as soon as possible.

On this Friday, even though we were supposed to leave Barcelona early afternoon, allowing ample time to make the three-and-a-half-hour trip by rental car before sundown, media inquiries interceded, jeopardizing the entire trip. We decided to go anyway.

Minutes after we finally set out, Esperanza, apparently still in journalist mode, began interrogating me about my unfinished novel. I bridled at her inquiries, as my unfinished book was a sore point, but she kept pestering me regardless.

"Come on, Leev," she pleaded from the passenger seat. "Tell

me again what it's about. I won't stop asking until you tell me, and we've got a long drive ahead."

"I told you, it's a kind of coming-of-age story. You write what you know. That's all there is to say about it."

"It's about you?"

"Sort of," I answered tersely, hoping to put an end to the discussion. Why ruin the festive atmosphere? Esperanza wouldn't be deterred.

"What do you mean?"

I sighed. "Really, do we have to go through this again?"

"Yes, we do," She responded, softening me up with a kiss.

"Okay, it's about this guy…"

"What's his name?"

"Jon."

"Why Jon?"

"I guess it has an everyman quality."

"Is he handsome?" Esperanza asked mischievously.

"Devastatingly," I replied, straight-faced. "Any woman would be *very* lucky to have him."

"Clearly this is a work of fiction," Esperanza parried. "Continue."

I paused in frustration. "Handsome Jon dislikes his job—"

"In New York?" Esperanza asked.

"No, he's a low-level bureaucrat in Washington. It's tedious work. He's going nowhere."

"So he quits his job, moves to Spain, and meets the beautiful woman of his dreams?"

I laughed. "Not sure yet. I've only written four chapters. Jon is still plodding away aimlessly. It can't continue, though.

Something's got to give. Maybe he'll write a book. Or maybe not. I'm not sure. Can we talk about something else?"

"Not yet," Esperanza replied. "Tell me more."

"There's not much more to say," I replied, throwing my hands up in frustration. "Jon's dismal. In addition to his dead end job, his romantic life is a disaster, and his family is selfish. The political environment also is lethal."

"Lethal?"

"Reactionaries blame the usual suspects—immigrants, blacks, Jews, et cetera—for what they see as the country's decline. Their champion is a crooked real estate tycoon who, despite inheriting his wealth and bankrupting his company multiple times, portrays himself as a savvy businessman. He shares little in common with his supporters, aside from his vulgarity and racism."

"Sounds familiar," Esperanza observed.

"Art imitates life, not just the reverse," I replied. "However, in my telling, the real estate tycoon is a thin-skinned bully, humorless bigmouth, and pathological liar. He's psychologically unstable, if not downright insane, and a sexual predator. On top of that, his ridiculous hair looks like an animal pelt. He cozies up to tyrants. Yet he wins the presidency. Fiction, in this case, is stranger than the truth."

"Oh, Leev, that's too much. People will suspend their disbelief for only so long. You'll lose all credibility. Good writing is more subtle than that."

"Maybe I'll tone it down if I ever get back to it."

"What's it called?" Esperanza asked.

"The book? I'm not sure yet. It's about big issues, like finding purpose in life, so I was thinking its title should have an existential flavor. I haven't figured it out yet."

"Can I read what you've written so far?"

"I'm not sure. It needs a lot of work. I don't understand why you're so interested in it, Es," I snipped, using my nickname for her. "Why is it so important to you anyway?"

Esperanza did not respond. I did not push the matter. We drove on for five minutes in silence before she finally spoke, announcing, "I did something you may not like."

"What?"

"I told Guillermo about you."

"What did you say?"

"I said I know an American…"

"Who's a dishwasher?"

"No, silly, an American who quit his job to write a novel."

"Why did you do that?" I asked, confused. It's not even true. I've made no progress on the book since I arrived."

"So, I exaggerated a bit. I told also told him about your professional background—your corporate job in Manhattan and tenure in government."

"What was the point of doing that? It's none of his business."

"It was a sales pitch. In fact, I've been pitching you for a while. A lot of interest exists in the U.S. presidential election, particularly since Schmidt announced his candidacy and with all the violence that has been going on lately, but we've got nobody covering it. We're don't have the staff. Which is where you come in."

"I don't understand," I said. "What's this got to do with me?"

"You could write about American politics."

"Me?"

"Yes, you," Esperanza replied. "You'd be perfect"

"That's a stretch, Es."

"No, it isn't!" Esperanza shot back. "I know how passionate

you are about what's going on in your country. You follow events intently."

"That doesn't mean I could write about them."

"Leev," Esperanza said, leaning in close, "you're a consummate spectator. You observe from a safe distance, revealing little about yourself. It drove me crazy at first. That's why we almost didn't work. I thought you were a robot. But the same curiosity, if channeled, could make you a great writer. A writer, after all, is an eyewitness—an eyewitness that commits observations to paper in ways that reveal life's essence. That's you."

I grasped Esperanza's hand. "That's very sweet, Es. But I don't understand what my shitty novel has to do with writing a politics column."

"It doesn't—mostly. I think you should do it because I think you'd be good at it. It would be meaningful. I think I've convinced Guillermo to give you a shot. It would be on a trial basis, of course. You'd have to prove yourself, and it wouldn't pay much. A small stipend for each column you wrote, probably nothing more."

"I can barely speak Spanish, so how can I be expected to write in the language?"

"Silly boy, you won't. Your pieces would be translated."

I paused in thought. "When did you do this?"

"Do what?" Esperanza inquired.

"Come up with this plan?"

"A while back. Guillermo wasn't enthusiastic at first. But the presidential campaign in America is becoming more alarming by the day, so there's a growing appetite for coverage about it. My scoop helped, too. It gave me credibility. I pushed really hard ever since. Leev, this a great opportunity. I believe in you. I really do."

After a long pause, I said, "Okay."

"Okay?"

"Yes, I'll give it try."

Esperanza screeched in delight and gave me a hug. "Oh, Leev, you won't regret this, I promise."

"Your readers might!" I replied.

Presently, Esperanza screamed. "Leev, where are we? We're going in the wrong direction!"

"Are we?" I asked.

"Yes, we were supposed to take the V-21 exit. Did we do that?"

"I don't think so. But that's your fault," I joked. "If you hadn't asked me about my stupid book…"

"Oh, silly boy, I only brought you along because I hate driving, and now look what you've done!"

We continued directionless on a two-lane coastal road for twenty minutes before Esperanza, pointing to a sign for a seaside resort, urged me to stop. I pulled into a small roundabout on the right-hand side permitting safe passage across the busy thoroughfare.

"Are you really sure you want to go there?" I asked as we waited for a break in the traffic. "I see Swedish, German, and even Japanese flags," I added, referencing the flagpoles at the resort's entrance, "but no American ones. Clearly this place doesn't like my kind."

Esperanza giggled. "Don't worry, I'll protect you," she joked.

When a gap emerged, we crossed the road and dipped underneath a train bridge, turning right onto a gravel road that ran for a hundred meters before bending toward the sea, which was visible in the distance. I let Esperanza out near a sign reading "Apartaments Javaica" and parked the car.

The modest resort comprised several whitewashed buildings large enough to house a few dozen guests, a water tower, and ordinary parking areas made up of corrugated steel atop concrete pillars. Linen hung from several clotheslines. The traffic from the nearby road was audible despite a barrier that ran along the resort's perimeter. On this late-spring day before the tourist season, the venue appeared vacant. I suspected it was closed for the off-season.

Five minutes later, Esperanza emerged from a small house that served as the reception office. "We're in luck, Leev. They've got a place for us."

"You really want to stay here?" I asked. "We could still make it to Valencia."

"Yes, but we'd get in late. This is quaint and cute, and it's near the beach. Let's stay the night here."

Her phone rang. "Guillermo?" she said into the receiver. A long pause ensued. "Hold on just one moment." Esperanza leaned over and, in a whisper, apologized for the interruption. "Walk down to the beach. I'll reserve a place and meet you there once I get off the phone."

As I turned to leave, Esperanza beckoned me back, kissing me on the cheek and snatching the Tigers cap I was wearing, placing it on her own head. "I'll tell him you're interested," she whispered.

I walked down a concrete path littered with carob trees' string-bean-like pods that, when dried, could be ground into a cocoa substitute. The path ran past a two-story block of apartments, also whitewashed and modest, and a pair of fenced-in tennis courts, beside which were several acres of fallow farmland.

Past the tennis courts, the sandy ground rose markedly, and over the crest appeared the majestic Mediterranean. The dark blue and vacant sea, a giant slab of linoleum, was eerily calm. Small waves cascaded gently against the beach, which was barren in either direction. A desultory breeze carried with it the smell of sea salt.

I walked barefoot on the soft sand in the direction of a boarded-up kiosk advertising refreshments and returned via the shore's edge, dipping my toes into the cold surf. I then walked down to my left for several hundred meters before retreating to my original spot. With no sign of Esperanza, I sat cross-legged facing the sea, taking in the placid tableau, refreshingly uninterrupted by life's normal distractions. No vessel was visible in any direction. I had the sea to myself.

The sound of the waves lapping the shore was lulling, and after several minutes, I closed my eyes and surrendered myself to the hypnotic symphony of the water's movement and the rhythmic shifting of sand and pebbles. As I descended into a wondrously calm, trancelike state, a sense of lightness enveloped me like a soothing mist. My breathing slowed. I felt airy, light.

In my mind's eye, I began to ascend slowly, rising about ten feet. From my new vantage point, I looked directly down on the slow rise and fall of my shoulders as I breathed. It was a familiar scene, replayed many times in the past in a hypnotic state, and I waited expectantly for the shrill wailing of an anguished baby, legs and arms kicking spasmodically, to appear in my place.

None appeared.

Below, I remained me—peaceful and intact. Minutes passed in harmonious tranquility, with no sign of the bawling infant. Eventually, I descended gently and reentered my seated self seamlessly, at which point I slowly opened my eyes, allowing the tranquil Mediterranean to again come into view.

I sat in gentle repose, gathering my thoughts, before standing up and stretching, as if having roused from a long slumber. With the sun beginning to set on the horizon, I decided to check on Esperanza. However, as I began to retrace my steps toward the resort, my phone rang. I did not recognize the number.

"Hello," I said.

"Liv, is that you?" my mother asked. "I've been so worried about you."

"Mom, it must be the middle of the night in California. Is everything okay?"

"Yes, everything's fine. I'm calling from Boston. Your father and I came here for a conference of his. Can you believe that I haven't been here in seventeen years? Seventeen years, Liv. That's how long! I'd forgotten what a delight the city is. It's so charming. Yesterday, in fact, your father and I walked around Faneuil Hall and the Common. We've had such great weather.

"Your father had a reception in the afternoon, so I took in the Museum of Fine Arts alone. It has a fabulous collection. I had no idea. It inspired me to get back into painting. To be honest, I'm still in a creative rut. One has to have a certain serenity to produce art, and ever since we relocated from Wisconsin, I have been acclimating to Southern California. Not that I realized this, since the area is so captivating. Yet somehow I've felt out of sorts. In fact…"

As my mother prattled on, Esperanza appeared over the crest at the path's end. Spotting me, she waved and then, unexpectedly, raised her hands above her head and walked toward me, slowly swiveling her hips as if doing an exaggerated impression of a catwalk model.

"Mom," I said, interrupting. "I have to go. I'm so sorry. I'll call you back. I promise."

"Oh, okay," she replied, crestfallen. "But do call me back soon. I have so much to tell you."

Approaching, Esperanza asked, "Who was that?"

"That," I said, "was my other Spanish girlfriend."

"Really? What's her name?" Esperanza said, wrapping her arms around me.

"Umm, Patricia."

"Patricia? Tell me about her."

"Well, if you must know," I started mischievously, "she's very attentive, not unlike another girlfriend of mine. However, Patricia cooks me paella every night, unlike another girlfriend of mine. And get this, she always praises my Spanish."

"This Patricia is quite special, but obviously not a native Spanish speaker."

"She is special," I affirmed, "but I still like my other girlfriend more."

"Oh, why's that?"

"If you must know, it's her punctuality. She's not like other Spaniards. She's always on time. For example, she never runs late for weekend getaways."

"Leev!" Esperanza guffawed, kissing me.

"It was my mother," I confessed. Esperanza flashed me a concerned look. "No, everything's fine. She's in Boston with my father. I'll call her back later. How is your other boyfriend?"

"Who's that?" Esperanza asked.

"Guillermo."

Esperanza laughed. "He's fine. He wants me to do some more interviews next week. He's convinced we can leverage the attention we've received to do a broader piece. He's thinking big. He's talking about a national-level report. I think he's gotten a little carried away. We'll have to see."

"That's fantastic!" I exclaimed, adding that a more extensive investigative report, on the heels of the one she had just completed, could make her career. This is what she'd been waiting for.

Esperanza quickly changed the subject, perhaps not wanting to risk jinxing things. "I brought up the possibility of you writing a few columns on a trial basis. He seemed enthusiastic."

"That's very kind of you, Es," I said, kissing her. "You know…"

"What's that?" she answered, peering into my eyes.

"Es, you're my…"

"I'm you're what, silly boy?"

"Es," I began again, "you're my…my…happy delusion."

Esperanza looked at me in confusion, her expression vacant. After a few moments, though, her eyes moistened and came alive. "Leev," she whispered, kissing me, "I…"

She embraced me.

"Leev," she said finally, "I love you."

"I love you, too," I answered, gripping Esperanza's petite body tightly.

I closed my eyes and inhaled deeply, filling my lungs with the sweet ocean air, and then slowly exhaled, relinquishing in one long outbreath all unrequited expectations and encumbrances.

Over the horizon, a chaotic and inscrutable world whirred, sending sparks of mayhem in every direction. But here, in this moment, all was hopeful and serene. I turned my head toward the ocean and awaited eternity in its cinematic tides.

The world is a mighty beast that can easily devour you. Yet, as I embraced Esperanza, I thought of all possibilities instead of obstructions, and that my survival and my happiness were self-configured, and I reassembled accordingly. I was, it struck me, a work in progress. Such is the tenuous fate of all who travail this small planet.